BLOOD STONE

A JOHN JORDAN MYSTERY

MICHAEL LISTER

PULPWOOD PRESS

Paperback ISBN: **978-1-947606-03-6**

BLOOD STONE

1

I was sitting on a barstool in Scarlett's trying to act less drunk than I was when Frank Morgan walked in.

It was 1988, the one hundredth anniversary of the Jack the Ripper case, and my third year in Atlanta.

A small crowd of regulars were spread around the bar. George Michael's Father Figure was on the jukebox, but I seemed to be the only one listening. A chilly October wind whistled outside and found cracks and crevices to enter Scarlett's and make her cold and drafty.

Behind me on a small table in the back corner were textbooks I was supposed to be studying, but I was finding it difficult to focus.

I had stepped over to the bar to ask Susan for a kiss and another vodka cranberry, which she was busy making because she didn't know about the two I had before I arrived, or the one her Aunt Margaret slipped me when she wasn't looking.

Margaret, like me, was a functioning alcoholic—though I wasn't sure how well either of us was actually functioning. Of course, functioning is a relative term, and addicts like us love few things as much as equivocation.

Margaret used not to drink as much as she does now. At least that's what I'd been told. But that was back before—before she'd lost the reasons not to. Before Laney Mitchell, the love of her life, died and left her alone with the Gone with the Wind-themed bar they had started together during happier times.

Like Margaret herself, Scarlett's had fallen on hard times, the faded and dust-covered book-and-movie memorabilia more sad than anything else.

Susan handed me my drink and before taking so much as the first sip I knew it would be heavy on the cranberry and light on the vodka.

"Thanks," I said, adding, "Wait" when she turned away to open a bottle of Bud for the old gray regular across the way.

"What?"

"You forgot my kiss."

"Oh. Sorry."

She bounced back over, and placing both palms on the bar, pushed herself up and kissed me.

When I tried to respond with a similar energy and enthusiasm I turned my glass over, splashing its contents all over the wooden bar top.

"Man down," I said. "Damn it, man."

A flush of embarrassment and self-consciousness joined the vodka blush I already had going.

I never felt as weak or pathetic as when I was drinking—and never practiced as much self-loathing—neither in volume nor vitriol.

"I'll get it," she said. "Just go sit down and I'll bring you and Frank a drink."

I turned toward Frank who was walking up.

"What're you drinkin', Frank?" I said. "Let me buy you a drink."

He held his hands up, palms out. "I'm good. Thanks though."

"Come on, man. Don't make me—don't be like that."

He nodded and gave a little frown of resignation. "A beer. I'll have a beer."

"Any particular kind?" I asked.

"Ah," he said, looking around, his eyes coming to rest on the Budweiser pendants hanging above the bar. "I'll have a Budweiser."

"The king of beers," I said. "Excellent choice. Draft or bottle? Margaret runs a full service drinkery here. She's no slouch."

Frank looked at Susan, who had drifted back over in our direction after passing out a few bottles and collecting the cash payments from guys who would become belligerent about their bills later.

There were no tabs at Scarlett's.

"Surprise me," he said. "No, you know what. I'll take a draft."

"You got it. How are you, Frank?"

"I've been better, but it's good to see y'all."

"You too," she said. "Always."

"Mind if I borrow your young man for a few minutes?" he asked.

"He's all yours. I'll be over in a minute with your drinks."

"Step into my office," I said, and stumbled back over toward what had come to be known as my table.

"How are you?" he asked as he sat down.

I nodded emphatically. "Really good. Things are great. You?"

I sounded like I was trying to convince myself as much or more than him, but neither of us was.

"Not so good."

"What's—"

"What're you—"

"You first," I said.

He looked down at my books. "What're you taking this semester?"

"Hebrew. Hebrew Prophets. And Biblical Interpretation. Have an exam on the prophets tomorrow."

He nodded. "That's good. Glad you got back in school and are doing so well. I'm proud of you."

"Why are things not so good for you?" I asked. "You working the three missing girls?"

He nodded again. "It's four now. Another went missing last night. But how'd you know they were connected? Nothing in the papers to suggest we think they're—"

"Just read the accounts and connected the dots," I said.

"What dots? There were no dots."

Susan arrived with our drinks. A Bud draft for Frank. A cup of coffee for me.

"Ah, Miss, this isn't what I ordered," I said.

"It's the only drink we have for underage drinkers," she said and moved away before I could argue with her about it. Glancing over her shoulder she added, "Especially when our favorite GBI agent is on the premises."

"Cheers," Frank said and held out his glass.

"Cheers," I said, white porcelain clinking shaker glass.

I took a sip of the strong, black, unsweetened liquid and had the urge to spit it back into the cup, but swallowed it instead. "That is truly horrific," I said and turned up the cup and quickly downed the rest of the tepid drink as if it were a shot, trying not to taste it as I did.

"How'd you know the three women were connected?" he asked.

"They were all runners or—"

He shook his head. "Reports didn't say that and they're—"

"Paper said the first one was a runner," I said. "The subtexts of the other stories along with the pictures included indicated the other two were athletic, in shape. I assume all three either ran or walked and were abducted while they were out doing it. All three are of similar age, body type, backgrounds. All have a similar look. Is the same true of the fourth?"

He nodded and sighed. "Yeah. And you're right. They're

runners. Went missing while out for a run. The doer's got to be in great shape. We're talkin' seriously athletic women."

"That's probably part of what does it for him," I said. "The challenge. The risk. Hunting what he considers a worthy prey. Plus he likes hard bodies. He has a type. Definitely got a serial on your hands."

"But a serial what?" he said. "What's he doing with them? Raping? Collecting? Killing? If he's killing 'em where're the bodies? If he's collecting them . . . where's he keepin' them?"

"He's got his own place," I said. "With plenty of room to work and or cage them. Or you just haven't found his dumping ground yet."

"How would you like to help us find them—and him?"

Frank had always been supportive of my interest in investigative technique. He had facilitated my work on the Atlanta Child Murders, even though to him and the other members of the task force the case was closed. He had helped me more than I could even calculate on the LaMarcus Williams and Cedric Porter cases. He had allowed me to work on a few of his cases with him and had even made it so I could take the training and get certified in law enforcement. Perhaps best of all, he had made it possible for me to attend some of the special FBI training at a few of their road school programs at various agencies in the area.

He was also the closest thing I had to a dad in Atlanta—maybe anywhere since my fractured relationship with my own father was still strained.

"How?" I asked, a jangle of electricity humming through me.

"Join the task force. You'd actually become an officer with one of the little towns around here—whoever has an opening. I'm still working out all the details. The job itself won't be anything special. You'll start out as a uniform, but you'd be on special assignment, working this case. You could stay in school, but you'd have to quit your job."

My jobs—janitorial work at the college and delivering Domino's pizza—were an embarrassment, and if he didn't know what they were I wasn't about to tell him.

"You've got a gift—think about how you connected the cases. We could really use it on this thing. Plus you're in shape. You still running?"

I nodded. Since I had stopped playing basketball because of what happened to Martin, I had started running.

"If this thing comes down to a footrace maybe you could actually catch the bastard. I'm not sure anyone else on the task force could."

"What happens when this thing ends?" I asked. "What if we catch him tomorrow?"

"You'd still be an officer with whichever PD we get you on with. Put in your time there and then you can transfer to Atlanta PD, one of the county sheriff's departments, or join me at GBI. It's all already arranged. All you have to say is yes."

"Yes."

"Yes?"

"Hell yes."

"You don't need to talk to Susan first?" he asked.

I shook my head.

"When can you start?"

"How about now?"

2

I let myself into Cheryl Carver's apartment off of Wesley Chapel with the key Frank had given me, one of Frank's .45s in a holster on my hip, a penlight in one hand, the case file in the other.

What I didn't have was any kind of official ID, so I was hoping not to have any encounters with family, friends, nosy neighbors, or a zealous superintendent investigating suspicious activity in a missing woman's apartment.

The small, dark dwelling smelled stale, as if the still air trapped inside it hadn't been stirred in several days.

Beneath the staleness, the smells of everyone who had ever lived here lingered—layered, pungent, contradicting, steeped in the carpet, baked into the sheetrock, soaked into the linoleum.

Barely bigger than a studio, the tiny one-bedroom unit consisted of a small living room, a tiny kitchen and eating area, a prison-cell-sized bathroom, and a bedroom not large enough to accommodate even a queen-size bed.

And though there wasn't room for much furniture in the sad, desperate little quarters, there was room for far more than she had.

A single, old couch with a bunched and gathered slipcover on it was the only object in the living room. No TV. No coffee table. No chairs. No end tables.

A single framed photograph hung on the wall—a dime store or church directory family portrait portraying Cheryl and her younger brother with her folks, all of them dressed up, each coordinating with the other.

According to the file, Cheryl was from a small farming community in South Georgia and had moved to Atlanta for school, her track scholarship providing just enough to cover her classes, textbooks, and this minuscule off-campus apartment. A part-time job at Burger King provided both food and money for food.

A small folding card table with a single folding chair at it was in the dining area that fronted the one-cook kitchen.

The hallway leading to the bathroom and bedroom was lined with running ribbons and medals—marathons, half-marathons, track and field competitions, 5Ks, 10Ks, 20Ks, gold, silver, and bronze medals, blue, red, and green ribbons, but mostly blue ribbons and gold medals.

Cheryl had been raised in poverty, but was running away from it as fast as her long legs would carry her.

The small bedroom at the end of the short hall held a little girl's white pressboard twin bed with a juvenile pink bedspread, which I suspected had come from Cheryl's childhood bedroom, probably packed in the back of her dad's pickup truck and driven up from South Georgia with her mom's promise to replace it just as soon as she could save up enough to do so.

A small matching dresser close by held her bras and panties and socks and t-shirts and pajamas, its bottom drawer reserved for newspaper clippings of her races, random pictures of family and friends, and various cards and letters—mostly from her mom.

Unlike the rest of the apartment, Cheryl's bedroom still had the hint of fragrant flowers in it. Perhaps it was her perfume or body lotion lingering from where it wafted around her before she left, or the homemade lavender sachets in her closet and dresser drawers.

Very few clothes hung in the closet, mostly faded Sears and K-Mart shirts and well-worn off-brand blue jeans, jogging suits, and athletic attire, the floor beneath them littered with tennis shoes and track cleats that had traveled many, many miles.

I searched the room, looking beneath the bed, behind the dresser, under and around and in everything. There was nothing hidden. Cheryl Carver had nothing to hide.

From every indication she was living a Spartan existence, partly because she had no other choice, but partly because she was a disciplined dogged athlete, a dedicated and determined student.

Unbidden, thoughts of my own excesses floated to the surface of my still not completely sober mind.

Cheryl Carver had nearly all of her adult life ahead of her, and she was investing toward making it a good one.

And then she had encountered a madman.

A sadistic, heartless, heretic of humanity who derived pleasure from pain.

And for some reason she had not been able to outrun him. Was it because of the nature of his attack? Did he surprise her? Did he pounce before she even had the chance to run? Or, like her, did he too run like he was designed to?

I sat on the edge of Cheryl's small bed and took in more of her room.

The small boombox beside her bed, the many cassettes and few CDs surrounding it. The stacks of textbooks on the floor, the smattering of romance novels mixed in. The Chariots of Fire one-sheet thumbtacked to an otherwise empty wall.

The sadness pressing down on me was overwhelming.

Why did the world have to be this way?

Why couldn't a gifted student and athlete go for a run without running into brutality and depravity?

"Where are you?" I asked, my voice sounding small and out of place in the quiet, feminine apartment. "Are you still in the land of the living? Are you his prisoner? Or in what wound in the earth are you buried?"

No response.

"I will find you," I said. "Either way. I promise you that. I'm gonna find the madman who did this to you too. I wish I could undo what he's done . . . but . . . it won't go . . . unpunished. You have my word."

3

Susan and I were living together in an old farmhouse off of Flakes Mill Road near Ellenwood.

Though most of the farm had been divided up and sold, the house still sat on ten acres and had a huge multi-car garage in the back, which the owner's son had built and filled with various sport cars in differing stages of restoration when he had lived here.

The house was small and drafty and had neither central air conditioning nor heat, but the rent was cheap, the rural feel refreshing, and it was less than five miles from the college I attended.

When I pulled into the small semicircle gravel drive, I could see that the lights were off in our bedroom, which meant Susan had already gone to bed.

I could feel the familiar agitation rising inside me, the tension gathering in my shoulders.

Most days this time of night when we both got home was our first and often only opportunity to spend time together and make love and she knew it. She not only knew that but knew how important it was to me. I was growing frustrated and more than a little angry at her take-it-or-leave-it, nonchalance approach to both our time alone together and lovemaking.

Instead of going to all four victim's homes, I had only gone to one—the one that was the closest to our home—so I could get here around the time she did. And she knew it. I had told her what I was going to do and why, and still she had gone to bed.

And once she had gone to bed, that was it. She wouldn't be getting up again. She wouldn't welcome a visit from me into our room. She was sending a message.

I wanted her every night, but tonight, after experiencing the overwhelming sadness and loss of Cheryl Carver, I needed her, needed the warmth, affection, and connection of human interaction and intimacy, needed to feel her live heart beating beneath her bare breasts.

Immediately I began to try and work out how much vodka I had hidden in the house.

I would read the case files and work my way toward oblivion.

A makeshift office in an alcove of the second bedroom created by placing bookshelves across the opening served as my small study and library, and tonight, investigative war room.

Case notes, photographs, and newspaper clippings spread out across my folding table desk, vodka in a coffee cup, orange juice in a glass for cover, and radio playing softly in the background—at the moment Whitney Houston's Where Do Broken Hearts Go.

The case file didn't yet contain any information on Kathy Dady, the fourth young woman to go missing, only Cheryl Carver, Paula Nichols, and Shelly Hepola.

The pictures I had of the three women showed just how alike they were. All tall, lean, athletic, attractive without being classically pretty. They wore little to no makeup and had a certain purity and plainness about them.

"You have a type, don't you?" I said aloud to the still faceless madman. "Why? Where does it come from? Do they all look like the same woman? Are you really doing this to her? Over and over again? Do you see her instead of them?"

As Whitney gave way to Richard Marx's Hold On to the Nights, the cold October wind found its way through the varnished boards of the old farm house, and I slid my chair a little closer to the space heater on the floor.

Wondering where the women were crossing paths with their abductor, I checked to see if they were all from the same area or had the same profession or frequented the same places.

Cheryl was a student in Decatur. Paula was a secretary in Marietta. Shelly worked retail in Duluth. They didn't go to the same gym or church or clubs. They didn't attend the same high school or college.

From what was in the file there was no obvious crossing, no intersection where the women would have encountered each other or the inexplicable madness that snatched them from their lives.

Two of the three women were single, and seemed not to have a lot of friends. They appeared to be introverts leading quiet lives.

Shelly had a boyfriend and he would have to be looked at closer, but if this was what it appeared to be, it was more likely a stranger than an acquaintance of any of the women. Of course, likely is not definitely.

When I became aware of the radio again, Phil Collins was singing Groovy Kind Of Love.

As I sipped my way toward stupor I wondered where the women were. Were we dealing with a collector or a killer? Either way, where were they?

Did he have a hidden dumping ground or a basement filled with cells or cages?

I still couldn't see his face, but if I knew which one he had, knew exactly what he was doing with his victims—rape? torture?

murder?—I'd have a better sense of him. At least that was what I told myself.

The next morning I woke to the sound of a loud alarm blasting George Harrison's I Got My Mind Set on You.

Which wasn't a bad song to wake up to.

I was still sitting in the chair from the night before, my head lying on my arms on the folding table that served as my desk.

Susan, who had already left for her other job, had brought the alarm clock in and placed it on the tabletop beside my head, which meant she had to unplug it, move it, plug it back in, then reset both the time and the alarm—all early this morning while trying to get ready and leave for work on time.

As I sat up, I felt not only like I had had too much to drink the night before but that I had slept sitting up in an old desk chair, my head on my folded arms on a table. I was stiff and sore, my head ached, my arms asleep.

But George's catchy, repetitive, remake compelled me to get up and get going.

Glancing around my small office space, I saw that Susan had straightened up some, returning the papers and photos to the case file, removing the cups and mostly empty vodka bottle, and picking up the various articles of clothing and shoes I had left on the floor.

Next to the case file were my textbooks and notebooks for class and a note that said she had made my lunch and left it in the fridge.

She was always doing things like this—things that provoked in me both guilt and gratitude.

I was flooded with shame and, not for the first time, wished I could skip ahead to be an older, wiser, better version of myself. I wanted to do better, to be better, and I knew I could, but I wasn't yet and it frustrated and embarrassed me.

Reaching over and tapping the Snooze button on the clock and silencing the song that would echo in my head all day, I pushed myself up and stumbled out of my office and into my day.

After driving over and running at Panola Mountain State Park, I found myself as I had far too often lately, at Jordan Moore's grave in Fairview Memorial Gardens, which happened to be less than a mile from my house.

The early morning sun had yet to burn the dew off the ground and the sweat on my body was quickly turning cold.

"I know I've got to stop coming," I said. "And I will. I know I will. I just don't know when yet."

As I looked at her headstone while I talked to her, I realized what an odd thing it was to do. Perhaps something of her body still remained beneath the earth, but the headstone had nothing to do with her or her life. And I couldn't help but wonder if I'd be better off going to some place we actually spent time together.

"Damn you for what you did," I said. "Damn me for still being hung up on you."

Miss Ida, Jordan's stepmom, stepped out from behind the stone statue of Saint Mark and said, "Goddamn the whole mess. Every last bit of it."

Ida Williams, a largish black woman perpetually in a traditional African print dashiki and head wrap, had a son who was murdered during the Atlanta Child Murders, and I had investigated it when I had first arrived in Atlanta back in '86. I had actually solved the case and figured out exactly what happened to little LaMarcus, but at a price I was still paying.

"Didn't realize you still came here," she said.

I nodded. "Just live up the road."

"Is she why?"

"Huh?" I asked, not following.

"Did you move out here to be close to her grave?"

I opened my mouth quickly, but nothing came out. I was unable to respond because I couldn't admit the truth and I couldn't lie to her.

"It ain't my business," she said. "I just care about you, boy."

"I'm not doing too good right now," I said. "But . . . I'm doing the best I can."

She nodded. "Same here," she said and paused a moment before adding, "All we can do."

"I . . . feel . . . so weak . . . so . . . I'm pathetic."

"You're neither of those," she said. "You're just hurting, son. Grieving. Give it some time."

"It's been some time already."

"Then give it some more. What else you gonna do? What the hell else any of us gonna do?"

4

Kathy Dady, the fourth young woman to go missing, lived in a small house she had inherited from her grandmother in the little town of Stone Mountain.

Frank and I met two Stone Mountain uniformed officers to take a look at her place.

"What's really going on?" Walt Thurman asked Frank as we walked up.

Thurman was a youngish, muscular black man with light skin and eyes of about the same color and a very slight mustache above large lips and small teeth with slight space between them.

We were standing out in the front yard of Kathy Dady's little house with him and his partner, a female cop named Erin Newman.

"Whatta you mean?" Frank asked.

"Why is GBI interested in a missing person who's only been missin' two days?"

"We're trying to keep a lid on this thing," he said, "so don't say anything, but we think her disappearance could be connected to some others in the metro area."

"Other missing women?" Erin Newman said.

Frank nodded.

Newman was a tall, thin woman with longish dishwater blond hair and a plain, longish face with too much makeup on it. She wasn't as awkward as she should've been given her size and build, but the uniform didn't do her any favors.

Frank nodded again. "We believe so, yes."

"They're all in the same age range, have the same body type and look," I said. "And we think they're all active in the same way —runners or walkers. Something like that."

"This is John Jordan," Frank said.

"No way you're GBI," Walt said. "Are you even out of high school yet?"

"John's gonna be helping us with this one," Frank said. "I've worked with him before and he's good. Really good. He's still a college student, but he'll be on the task force."

"Task force?" Walt said.

"Yeah, but keep it quiet. We really don't want this out yet."

"What's the age range?" Erin asked.

"Nineteen to twenty-six so far," I said.

"Anything else link them?"

"Not that we've found so far," Frank said.

"How long's it been going on?" she asked.

"A few months," Frank said. "First woman disappeared at the end of August. There was more time between the first and second than the second and third and more time between the second and third than the third and fourth."

"So he's speeding up," she said.

"Yes he is."

"Are all the victims still missing?" she asked. "No bodies found or anything yet?"

"Yeah. Right. No bodies yet."

"So they could still be alive," she said.

"That's the hope," Frank said. "Let's take a look inside and see if Kathy's place can tell us anything that'll help."

Kathy Dady's inherited house was overfilled with old furniture and collectable knickknacks—porcelain dolls and keepsakes and mementoes and salt and pepper shakers. Thousands of them.

"I'd say she hasn't changed the place much since it was her grandmother's place," Erin said.

"Sure still smells like grandma's house," Walt says. "What is it about old people and mothballs? My granny's house smell the same way."

"Mrs. Dady only died about three months ago," Frank said. "Hasn't been Kathy's place long."

We moved slowly and carefully through the small rooms of the small house, examining things that may or may not have been a reflection of Kathy at all.

Several times I had to stop myself from whistling or humming I've Got My Mind Set on You.

Random cat hairs were strewn about, but there was no cat. No cat food. No bowl. No litter box.

Most of the furniture was painted white. None of it was nice. All of it was old, but not antique.

The two main accent colors were mauve and country blue, but the walls and ceilings and drapes and furniture were white.

In what must have been her grandmother's bedroom, nothing had been disturbed. I'd have bet my rent money that it was just as it was on the day Mrs. Dady died.

In the guest room we found an open suitcase on the floor with clothes spilling out of it.

"Kathy's obviously staying in here," Erin said.

"Sort of a slob, ain't she?" Walt said.

"Look," I said to Frank, nodding toward the pairs of running shoes and athletic socks.

"She's definitely a runner," Erin said. "Lots of jogging suits and gym shorts too."

"What made you first conclude they were runners?" Frank asked me.

"After reading that the first one was and seeing how athletically built and active they all were, and hearing they weren't abducted from their homes, I figured they were all out doing a similar activity—walking or running—when they were taken. It's an activity mostly done alone and one that leaves them more vulnerable than most things they do."

He nodded. "That's mostly what we came up with, but it took a while and it was a group of highly trained and experienced investigators."

"What's your story?" Erin asked me.

I shrugged. "Don't have much of one yet, but I'm working on it."

"He's being modest," Frank said. "You familiar with the LaMarcus Williams and Cedric Porter cases? He solved them. Both. On his own."

I shook my head. "It wasn't on my own."

"Sure, okay, but you . . . it was you who connected the dots, figured them out, and brought down the killers."

"Pretty impressive for someone who looks like they're still in high school," she said. "If you ever need a place to work, we have an opening on our force. And you can tell from looking at me and Walt that our chief is all about diversity."

5

As we drove through the little town of Stone Mountain—shops on one side of the street, railroad tracks and old depot on the other—Frank was talking, but his words had become as desultory to me as the sounds of the train and traffic.

Everything outside of me had faded, receded into a dim semi-silent background.

I was thinking, my sober mind concentrating on connections, shifting around the various pieces of information in the case as if parts of a complex puzzle for which the box and therefore the picture had been lost.

I've Got My Mind Set on You tried to work its way into my consciousness, but I sent it back to the old jukebox in the basement it had come from.

Why am I still set on Jordan? Why can't I feel for Susan the way I did for Jordan, the way I still do for Anna?

Who is your mind set on? Who is the pattern for all these women? Who are you taking, dominating, controlling over and over and over again?

I thought about the women again. Was something besides running connecting them? Was I missing something?

They had caught his eye, but how? Where?

And then a thought.

"What if—" I started, but realized Frank was still speaking.

"What if what?" he asked.

"I was just thinking about where he might be seeing them," I said. "What if he's selling them their running shoes or sports bras or jogging suits or something?"

He nodded vigorously. "That's good. I like that. That might just be—"

"He's seeing them somewhere," I said. "If running is what's connecting them . . . makes sense he'd see them somewhere associated with that."

"Sure," he said. "Let's say he works in a sporting goods store. He'd see hundreds of women, but only certain ones would catch his eye."

"And for those . . . Let's say they sign up for a newsletter or . . . to get information about upcoming sales or to receive coupons . . . He'd have their addresses. We need to go through their mail, their receipts. See if they shop at the same store or are on the same newsletter or are a part of the same running group. Something's got to connect them."

"I'll get somebody on it this afternoon. Shouldn't take long. We should know something soon. Great work. Really good. How does it feel to be working a case again?"

I nodded. "Good. Real good. Thanks for . . . letting me."

We came to an intersection and stopped at a red light. He glanced around. "Nice little town," he said. "How would you feel about joining the department here?"

I shrugged. "Truth is . . . I'd be happy to be in any department. Anything would beat cleaning toilets and delivering pizza."

"The chief is an old friend of mine. Sounds like they need somebody and he'd be a good mentor. He's a good and decent man. Good, honest cop."

I wanted to tell him that I already had the best mentor possible, tell him how much I appreciated him, but I hesitated and the moment passed.

The red light changed to green and we continued forward again.

"What'd you think of Walt and Erin?" he asked.

"Liked them both. Really liked the way her mind worked. She asked some great questions. And he had no problem asking you just what the hell GBI was doing in his backyard on a recently missing person."

He nodded. "That's Bud. Guarantee he's trained 'em to be that way. Took their strengths and helped hone them. He'd do the same for you."

"That the chief?"

"Yeah. Bud Nelson. I'll give him a call as soon as I get back to the office. Or, hell, I could turnaround and we could go talk to him in person right now. What time is your class?"

"Half an hour," I said, "ago."

"Oh. Sorry. I'll get you back to the school, then go get a team started on the missing women's mail and receipts, then I'll call Bud."

"Thanks for all you're doing for me," I said.

"You kidding? You've already done more for the case than . . . anything I'll do for you."

It wasn't true, but it was exactly the kind of thing I'd come to expect him to say.

6

The ringing phone shattered the silence of the still, empty house.

Susan was working the evening shift at Scarlett's, and I was home alone.

Instead of delivering pizza, I was home. Instead of doing a Hebrew assignment, I was studying the case file.

It had still been daylight when I had come home from my afternoon classes and my janitorial job at the college, and I had come straight into my office and begun poring over the file.

Since then daylight had surrendered to dark, and as I stood to go answer the phone, I realized the small desk lamp in my office was the only light on in the entire house.

I also realized I had forgotten to turn on the heaters.

The quiet, lifeless house was dark and cold.

The only phone jack in the old house was in the kitchen, which was where the phone was—mounted to the wall, an extra-long cord between the base and the receiver allowing for movement around the kitchen and partly into the dining room.

On my short walk to the kitchen I not only realized that the house was dark and cold, but that I was hungry and, most surprising of all, I hadn't had a drink.

I snapped on the light in the small kitchen and snatched up the receiver.

As I had hoped, it was Frank.

"Got good news and bad news," he said. "I'll start with the bad. We've gone over receipts, phone records, mail . . . everything we can get our hands on . . . and there's no store or club or gym or anything we can find that the women have in common. Not a thing."

"Damn it," I said. "Really thought that could be it."

"It was a good thought. I was sure it was gonna be it too."

"And the good news?"

"Spoke with Bud Nelson this afternoon. You start to work for him tomorrow."

"Really? Thanks, Frank. Thank you so much."

"My pleasure," he said. "But I'm doing him the favor. You'll be a tremendous asset for his department. Just afraid there won't be much to use your gifts on, but . . . it's a good enough place to start."

"How are you choosing them?" I asked the madman.

Though talking to myself in a dark empty farmhouse made me look like I was the one who was mad.

I had turned on the heaters and was now moving through the house, clicking on a light here and there, thinking about the case, questioning the faceless monster at the center of this madness.

"I know you're not just driving around in a van looking for them. They're too specific, too matching of your type. So how? Where do you encounter them? Where do they catch your eye?"

Do you go to them or do they come to you?

How? When? Where?

I pictured the crosshairs of a rifle scope moving about and the victims running into it.

Running.

Does this even have anything to do with running? Am I wrong about that?

I thought about the role of running in my life and what I most liked about it.

For me it was meditation, a mental, emotional, and spiritual practice as much as a physical one.

At times running was euphoric, a stuporless oblivion.

Past the effort, past the sweat and pounding and pain, a certain and singular pleasure waited.

What state on the spectrum between pain and pleasure were the missing women in when the predator had leapt out of the darkness and snatched them out of the experience, out of their existences?

And as my mind flashed back to my run at Panola Mountain that morning, another thought came to me.

What if they all run in the same place? At least sometimes. What if sometimes they drive to the same place to run and that's where he sees them, where he snatches them?

What if he doesn't go to them? What if they come to him?

Where do people run?

Panola Mountain Park, obviously. Where else?

Piedmont Park.

The Chattahoochee River Trail.

This last one made me think of Wayne Williams, the Atlanta Child Murders, and the bodies pulled from the river.

Not now. Where else?

Maybe a particular stadium or track? Perhaps one of the metro area high schools opened their track to all runners at certain times and they all went to it.

And then it came to me. And when I thought it I knew it was the place.

Stone Mountain.

It's convenient. It's beautiful and peaceful. It has over three thousand acres of extraordinary natural beauty and miles and miles of roads and trails to run.

It's one of the most popular spots to walk and run and exercise in the entire area—perhaps the most popular.

Kathy actually lived in Stone Mountain near the park and the others were close enough to drive to it.

Now I just had to find out if they did.

I ran to my office to grab the file, then to the kitchen to the phone.

I found Shelly Hepola's boyfriend's name and number in the file and punched in his number.

"Hello."

"This Benton Weston?" I asked.

"Who wants to know?"

"My name is John Jordan. I'm with the GBI. We're looking into Shelly's disappearance."

"Oh. Yeah. Okay."

"Got a minute to answer a couple of questions?"

"Okay."

"Was Shelly a runner?"

"Yeah. Already told y'all that."

"Where would she run?" I asked. "Did she have any regular places she really liked?"

"Yeah, I guess. I don't know. She ran everywhere."

"Piedmont Park?"

"Yeah."

"Panola Mountain Park?"

"Yeah, I think. But not often."

"How about the Chattahoochee Trail?"

"Not so sure about that one. Don't think so."

"How about a school track or one of the college or pro stadiums?"

"Nah. Nothin' like that."

"Stone Mountain?"

"All the time. More there than anywhere else."

As soon as we hung up, I called Frank back.

"They're coming to him," I said when he answered.

"Huh?"

"He's not going to them. They're coming to him. He's not stalking them. He's stalking an area. At least I think he is. I talked to Benton Weston. Shelly's boyfriend. She ran there. Now we just have to see if the others did."

"Where?"

"Stone Mountain."

"Place is always full of runners and walkers," he said. "And all that woods . . . He could grab them, pull them into the woods, and . . . rape, kill, bury, who knows what all . . . right there."

"Exactly," I said. "I mean, it's just a theory, but . . . if they all ran there . . . and chances are good that they did . . ."

"It's a great theory and one we can quickly and easily confirm. We'll call family, friends, classmates, coworkers—anyone who might know—of all the missing women and find out. Great work, John. I'll be in touch."

7

I knew Frank was going to have agents contacting those who knew the missing women to see if they regularly ran at Stone Mountain, but that would most likely be the next day and I couldn't wait.

Going back to the file and using the metro area phonebook we had, I began tracking down anyone who might know where the young women ran.

It wasn't easy.

Several of the calls I made were to people who either didn't know the missing women or didn't know them well enough to know where they ran.

It took a while. And the entire time I was either standing in or walking around the kitchen.

The kitchen, like the rest of our rented farmhouse, looked like a poor young couple lived in it. We had little in the way of furniture and decorations—and nothing nice. The mismatched appliances weren't ours, only the few dishes, plates, pots, pans, and glasses—none of which were part of a complete set. Our mostly empty fridge looked like one in a frat house—random condiments and takeout containers.

Eventually I was able to reach the right person for each of the young women.

Cheryl's college track coach, a coworker of Paula's, Shelly's boyfriend, of course, and a friend of Kathy's—all confirmed that the women often ran at Stone Mountain.

Of course, they ran other places too, but Stone Mountain was the only running site that all the victims had in common.

When I finally finished, I started to call Frank, but thought better of it when I glanced at the time.

A little while later when Susan got home, I was still riding the rush of working the case, coming up with another theory, and confirming it.

I still hadn't eaten or had a drink—and was feeling particularly proud about the latter.

I wanted to talk to her about my day. I wanted to make love and hold each other. I wanted us to go get something to eat.

But she was exhausted and in a bad mood and wanted to go straight to bed.

"You sure you can't stay up with me for just a few minutes?" I asked.

"It's been a long, hard day."

I nodded. "I know. But maybe a little time together would make you feel better."

"Do you mean sex? You mean having sex, don't you? I'm just not up for it. I'm sorry. I just can't tonight."

"I want to make love, yes, but—need to, really—but I wasn't just talking about that. I meant just spend some time together. Even a little. We don't have to do anything but talk or hold each other."

"I can't even hold my eyes open. I just . . . it's better if I just go to bed."

And just like that I went from elation to frustration, from excitement to anger, from feeling happy and hopeful to feeling down and dejected.

With Susan in bed and our bedroom door closed, I paced around the house trying to decide what to do—where to put all the energy and excitement I had, what to do with all the anger and frustration.

Go for a run?

Have a drink?

Go for a drive?

Do homework?

Read the case file some more?

I decided to go pay Shelly Hepola's boyfriend a little visit.

"You look too young to be with the police," he said.

Unlike Shelly or any of the other missing women, Benton Weston III looked like money. He had answered the door of his expensive apartment wearing expensive clothes and an expensively dismissive expression on his face.

"I get that a lot," I said.

His thick, dark hair was longish and slicked back with gel or mousse or something, and he smelled of an expensive aftershave I associated with high-end department stores and country clubs. His clothes had the look and label of money, as did the furnishing filling the spacious apartment behind him.

He narrowed his small, slanted green eyes and looked up as if trying to figure out what to say. "Did y'all find her? Is she okay?"

That's it, I thought. Had to search for it, but you came up with the right questions to show concern.

I shook my head. "No news yet. Just stopped by to ask you some questions."

"At ten o'clock at night?" he said, his tone filled with disapproval and disdain.

"Tried to get here sooner, but . . ."

It was difficult to tell how old he was. My guess was somewhere between twenty-five and thirty. Whatever his age it was too young to afford a place like this with his own money.

"You got some sort of ID?" he said.

"Not on me, no," I said.

"Really? You serious? Who are you really?"

I felt stupid and embarrassed. This was an impulsive and ill-advised thing to do, and now I looked juvenile and stupid.

"I didn't know I was coming by. I've been off several hours. I just—"

"You a reporter? Or are you the sick fuck who took her? I'm calling the police."

"Look," I said, pulling out my wallet and holding it up. "Here's my ID."

"That's a fuckin' Florida driver's license," he said.

"That's where I'm from. Haven't changed it yet. Look at my ID. Then look at me. My name is John Jordan. Now, here's the card of the GBI agent in charge of Shelly's case. See it? Take it. His name is Frank Morgan. Close and lock the door. I'll stay right here. Call him and ask him who I am and if it's okay to talk to me. Okay? I just want to ask you a few questions. I'm trying to find Shelly. That's all. Call Frank Morgan and ask him. I'll be right here."

He looked back and forth from the card to me for a few moments, then nodded, and closed and locked the door.

It seemed like it took longer than it should have, but I stood there waiting, wondering if when he opened the door again it'd be with a knife or a gun.

I doubted he could be the abductor. Whatever was happening to the women, it was highly unlikely that one of their boyfriends did it to her and then to a series of other women also. Except they all looked like her, could be her to him. I couldn't count him out, though he lived in an apartment, so he certainly couldn't be a collector—not here at least. Of course, it was a big apartment, so . . . maybe.

When he opened the door again, the chain was on it.

Handing me Frank's card through the slight opening, he said, "Agent Morgan said it was okay to talk to you, but if I'd rather we could do it at his office with my attorney. And I'd rather. So . . ."

"Okay. No problem. I'm just trying to find Shelly. You want to delay that, fine, that's on you, but it's suspicious and makes me wonder why you would do it—like maybe you don't care or you already know where she is, maybe even have something to do with it. You have a good night now. I'll see you at the formal interview."

8

Wound up from what I had found out about the case and angry and frustrated from my interactions with Susan and Benton, I drove to Stone Mountain to run.

The night was cold. The wind was biting. I didn't care.

I really didn't have my running gear. I didn't care.

I ran in jeans, an inadequate jacket, and an old pair of basketball shoes I found in the trunk.

Looming large in the distance, Stone Mountain glowed eerily in the night sky, its granite surface a light gray-green.

Of all the unique and stunning features of Stone Mountain, perhaps what stood out the most was its vast barrenness. It's a 1,686-feet-high bare rock dome five miles in circumference. A geological marvel over three hundred million years in the making.

The night was dark, no moon or stars visible, the only illumination on the sidewalk I was running on came from periodic street lamps, and the spill from the mountain on one side and the inn on the other.

The famous face of the mountain was lit at night by a bank of large halogen lights mounted near the museum, but they were too weak to do anything but show a swath of the north face that included the carving of the three confederate figures from the Civil War. Even the part that was lit looked more like a mirage than anything else, and the rest of the giant granite mountain appeared more figment than reality.

Across the street from the mountain, its museum, gift shop, and sky ride, the Stone Mountain Inn's many lights also helped lessen the darkness in this area, but not by much.

I was here not so much to investigate—though it was extremely helpful to see what it was like to run here at night—but because I was going to run somewhere, so why not here.

I wasn't concerned about the madman. He had a very particular type, and I wasn't it. His was a most precise pattern so singular he was abducting the same woman over and over and over again.

As I ran I wondered why he had chosen this place.

Because of the mountain itself? Was it significant?

Because of the traffic? The thousands and thousands of potential prey to choose from?

Because of the location? Did it just come down to how convenient it was?

Or was it something else entirely? Something only significant deep down in the mind of madness?

I ran as hard and fast as I could.

I ran without stretching or warming up.

I ran until I felt better.

I ran until much of the anger and frustration and excess energy had dissipated.

I ran until I ran into Summer Grantham.

We were headed in different directions. I was running. She was walking. And we rounded a corner at the same moment.

"Are you okay?" I asked before I realized who I had just collided with.

"Yeah, I'm—" she began, then stopped abruptly. "John?"

Summer Grantham was a forty-something blond-haired brown-eyed psychic, though she didn't care for that term, with the youthful bearing and body of a teenager, a casual, unassuming manner and a gentle, nurturing nature. We had both been in the Missing and Murdered Children group for a while and had even dated for a time.

We embraced.

"What're you doing out here?" I asked.

"Just out for a walk," she said. "What about you? What are you running from?"

I laughed. "Too much to name."

She nodded and smiled warmly.

"I find it hard to believe you're just out here for a walk," I said.

"Any more than you're just out here for a run," she said. "Remember what I told you before? I go where I'm led."

She had told me that back when I first asked her why she was involved with the Missing and Murdered Children group. It was how she used her gift and lived her life—following impressions, leadings, going with her intuitions and attractions.

"I'd be very surprised if we're not out here for the same reasons," she said.

"And what's that?"

She shrugged. "You tell me. I don't know exactly, but it's dark and mad and wicked, and lives and souls hang in the balance."

There was something hypnotic about Summer, and everything associated with her—even her words and the cadence of her voice. A touched soul, she had an essential dreamlike quality.

"What drew you to the mountain?" she asked.

"A madman," I said. "Someone's abducting young women. Four so far that we know of."

She nodded vigorously. "That's it. But he's not just abducting them. None of those poor souls are any longer in the land of the living."

9

"Can you tell anything else?" I asked. "Anything about the madman? The women?"

"Let's walk back toward my car and give me a few minutes to . . ."

Without another word, we turned and began to walk back in the direction I had come from and she was headed toward when we ran into each other.

I grew as quiet and economic with my motions as I could while still walking, and let her set the pace and gait of our return.

There was nothing spooky or otherworldly about the way Summer worked. She just seemed to turn her gaze within and await impressions.

I had never heard her describe herself this way, but the way I thought about it was that we all have antenna systems—hers was just more sensitive, more powerful, her instruments far more finely calibrated than most. And unlike most of us, she trusted her feelings, intuitions, impressions, gave them a weight and import not many people do.

She was walking very slowly, moving in an awkward, stilted

manner. I was trying not to get in her way. I was also trying to make sure she didn't trip or walk into anything.

Eventually, she slid her arm around mine and closed her eyes, and I led her down the dark, intermittently lit sidewalk while she focused on her inner explorations.

I continued to let her set the pace. I just concentrated on keeping her on the sidewalk.

It took us a while, but eventually we made it back around to the north face of the mountain and the inn, to more illuminations and signs of life, then down another hill and up a small road cutting back at an angle behind the inn to where our vehicles were parked.

"They're still here, John," she said when we arrived at her car and she opened her eyes.

She was still driving a beige '68 Volkswagen Beetle that made me think of Ted Bundy.

"Do you know where?" I asked.

She shook her head. "It's . . . I can't quite get a . . . It's confusing. They seem to be in different places. And . . . it's like . . . two of them are suspended somehow. I don't know. It feels like purgatory. Like they're . . . It's like they're—I get the sense that they're all here, and yet two of them almost seem to be floating or . . . like they don't have a connection to the ground or earth. It's hard to explain. And I could be wrong about it. It's just the feeling that I'm getting. And it might not be literal or physical. It could be about their spiritual or emotional state. I just don't know."

I nodded and patted her arm, which I was still holding. It was like I felt a certain energy in our connection and I didn't want to break the circuit yet.

"They suffered, John. Not . . . physically so much—I'd say he isn't torturing them or doing anything especially sadistic—but . . . the mental anguish and . . . sheer terror of their final moments . . . is overwhelming."

I continued to nod, trying to take in everything she was conveying.

"Y'all've got to stop him. He won't . . . he can't stop himself. Someone else will have to do it. He couldn't if he wanted to and he doesn't want to. He . . . there's something ancient about what he's doing. He's . . . aware of . . . that aspect of it too. It's the only thing in his life that brings him any pleasure, any release of the enormous burden he labors around under."

"Burden? What kind of burden?"

"An existential one. The burden of someone like him just being alive."

"A lot of us would be more than happy to relieve him of that burden," I said.

"The chaos, loss, fear, and destruction he's unleashing is nothing to compare to what's inside him."

"Is there anything else you can tell me about him?"

"It's . . . this will sound obvious, but . . . it's even more so than you'd expect. The face he presents to the world is far different from his actual face. He's not what he seems at all. Not at all. He's like a . . . a skilled actor . . . playing a . . . playing the part of a lifetime."

10

The man touched with madness, the one who would soon come to be known as the Stone Cold Killer, wore what he thought of as a human suit. He put it on each morning along with his mask of sanity and work clothes.

He had always been good at pretending, at seeming to be other than what he was. He had to be to survive.

It had begun in childhood, this game of appearances.

His earliest memories were of being acutely aware of being different, alien, other. He wasn't like the other kids—the adults either for that matter, though they seemed foreign to all the kids. Back then he didn't yet know the intense pleasure of causing another pain. He just knew that the pain of others didn't trigger in him the same responses and feelings they did in other people.

He didn't know why he was unlike others. He just knew he was—and that if he was going to survive, even thrive among them, he had to fool them into believing he was one of them. And from that realization until this day, that was what he had done. The shroud of humanity he wore was his Trojan horse, he was the killer hiding inside. His mask of sanity was the sheep's skin, he was the wolf within.

Over time he had honed his skills, perfected his craft, and now appeared about as human as everyone else.

It hadn't been easy, but he had applied himself. Studying emotion and expression and empathy. Watching how people react, respond, interact. He had observed humans relating to each other like a researcher monitoring lab rats, noting the outward appearance of acceptable behavioral norms, committing to memory how to mock human beings to the point of seeming human himself.

Like certain actors he had heard interviewed, he did his best work at passing like everyone else when he was fully submerged in a character. Much more so than when he was himself pretending at normal emotions and social acceptability. So as an adult, he had always assumed an entire persona, completely submerging himself into the role of another—and the more different that other was from himself, the more convincing he could be. He could utterly vanish. All that would be left was what appeared to be an actual human being with actual humanity, complete with emotions and compassion, care and concern for other human beings.

Over the years, he had tried on a lot of different human suits, adopting the manner and appearance of a wide variety of humans, but his current concealment was by far his best, and he planned to stick with it for a long time to come.

And why wouldn't he? You don't abandon something working this well.

11

Bud Nelson wasn't what he appeared to be.

He was a middle-aged white man with a military manner, his gray hair cropped closely to his large head. He wore black slacks and a white shirt, both of which were ill-fitting and out of date, spit-shined black patent leather shoes, and black horned-rimmed glasses.

He looked like he belonged in the sixties, like he was part of the racist, sexist, oppressive old boys club, but in sharp contrast to his appearance, he was actually a kind, gentle progressive, who believed in and practiced equality in his small department.

"Welcome aboard, John," he said, shaking my hand. "Frank's told me good things. Look forward to having you on our squad."

"I'm happy to be here and honored to be working with you."

"You already met Erin and Walt," he said.

I nodded toward them, this police partner version of The Odd Couple. He was dark and squat. She was pale and tall, towering over him. They both wore tight navy blue turtlenecks beneath their uniforms, but his accentuated how large and bulldoggish his neck was, while hers drew attention to how long and giraffe-like hers was.

"This is Miss D, she runs the place. And this is Joe Ross—another patrol officer. You'll meet the others later."

We were all standing in the small squad room waiting for Frank and the other members of the task force to arrive.

Miss D, the secretary, was an older black lady with a short, small frame and long bony fingers. Joe Ross was a tall, quiet, awkward, late twenties white man who hunched his shoulders and was so skinny he looked concave.

There was something hayseedy and hickish about Joe—even before he opened his mouth and the extreme Southern drawl and bad grammar tumbled out.

His wispy hair was too long and in need of a haircut—or at least a wash, and he had questionable facial hair that was too short and patchy to be considered a beard and too slight to be considered stubble.

Along with his appearance, his slow, Southern drawl and good ol' boy manner, Joe Ross had been what I expected most of the department to be. It was impressive and said a lot about Bud that he was the exception, not the rule.

"Only three others," Walt said.

"All dispatchers," Erin said. "Very small department."

"Stone Mountain—the park," Walt added, "has its own police and fire departments. We're just a small town police force."

"Very small town," Erin added. "But it's a good town and a great department and a great place to start your law enforcement career."

"So let's get started," Bud said, "by catching this sick son of a bitch who's snatching our young ladies."

Frank arrived with a pale, chubby, blond haired man in his late twenties wearing a Stone Mountain Park police uniform.

"Sorry we're late," he said. "Been trying to coordinate everything."

I was sure he had been, but his stressed, unsteady manner and wrinkled and disheveled appearance suggested another reason too, and I remembered him saying he had been better the night he came in Scarlett's. I had jumped to the conclusion that it had to do with the missing young women, but maybe something else was going on with him as well. I needed to check on him when I could.

"This is Bobby Meredith. He'll be our liaison with the park police."

"Nice to meet you, Bobby," Bud said.

Bobby nodded but didn't say anything, and seemed less than enthusiastic to be here.

"Since it looks like all the young women were abducted from over here," Frank said, "the other agencies are going to let us handle it for now and have said we can call them in if we need anything."

"Where's the . . . ah . . . bathroom?" Bobby asked. "Had too much coffee this morning."

"Back of the . . . ah . . . hallway," Walt said, mocking the way Bobby had asked, though the doughy young man didn't seem to notice—either that or he didn't care.

After he was gone, Frank waited until he was in the restroom with the door closed before shaking his head and saying, "Park police are giving this a very low priority. Look who they assigned us. Say we haven't proved for sure that they went missing at the park and they don't want a word to that effect breathed. More concerned about visitors and tourists than anything else."

"Other agencies dropped out too?" Bud asked.

"More just backed off for now. They'll jump in if we need them. Missing persons isn't as sexy as murder or—probably best for now, anyway."

"You watch," Walt said, "we start turning up dead girls and they'll all come running—right alongside the media."

Bobby returned a moment later and we continued.

"What about public safety?" Erin asked. "Don't we have a duty to warn the young women coming out here to run?"

"That's exactly what we can't do," Bobby said. "Don't even know for sure that's what's going on. We can't cause panic over . . . a theory. If the park takes a hit, so does the town and the entire area. All our jobs would dry up and blow away in a heartbeat. We need to chill out and see what we've got first."

Ignoring him, she looked from Frank to Bud. "My question still stands."

"We're gonna be searching the park for any signs of the women or clues to their whereabouts," Frank said. "We'll be able to do more, to insist on more, once we have more to go on. In the meantime, we're beefing up security in the park and are gonna have extra patrols."

"Really seems like we should be doing more," she said.

I nodded. "I agree."

"I know," Frank said. "I feel the same way, but—"

Erin said, "What if we do a sting operation?"

She was looking at Bud now.

"I know I'm a little older," she continued, "but I'm built like the other girls and it's dark out there. What if I dressed like them and ran around the park at night? See if we can catch him? Stop him before he does it again?"

"What if he does it to you?" Frank said.

"I'm tough. I'm trained. I'll be armed. And I'll have backup."

"I like the idea," Bud said. "Beats sittin' around on our hands. Nobody tougher than Erin and we'll be right there with her."

"I don't know . . ." Frank said. "Seems . . ."

"How're you gonna feel when the next girl is taken if we didn't at least try?" she asked. "What will you tell her folks?"

"We'll take every precaution, Frank," Bud says. "She'll be fine. And we might just catch the bastard. Think we gotta try."

Frank frowned and seemed to think about it.

"I'll head it up while you oversee the search of the park," Bud said. "Who knows? Maybe we'll both get lucky."

12

As preparations were being made for the sting operation and a crime scene team searched the park for the missing women, Frank and I interviewed Benton Weston, Shelly's boyfriend.

He arrived at Frank's office with his father and two attorneys.

All four men had on expensive suits and ties and stylish overcoats. Benton Weston III looked a little and acted a lot like Gordon Gekko, but Benton II was no Bud Fox.

"Thanks for coming in," Frank said. "We really appreciate your help with this."

He was smiling and sounded genuinely grateful, not a hint of frustration or aggravation in his voice or bearing.

"We don't mind helping," Benton's father said, "we just hope it won't take long. I'm missing some important meetings to be here."

As if in uniform, all four men wore light blue dress shirts with white collars and suspenders.

"We'll get you out of here just as soon as possible," Frank said.

"Who is this young man?" one of the attorneys asked, nodding toward me.

"This is officer Jordan with the Stone Mountain Police Department. He's assisting with the investigation."

"He looks too young to be—"

"Okay," Frank said, cutting him off, "let's get started so we can get y'all out of here. Let's start with your relationship with Shelly."

Benton shrugged. "Wasn't much to it. Hadn't been together long. Wasn't serious. Before she went missing I was thinking about calling it off."

"Why's that?"

"To be honest . . . we were just too different. From different worlds. Ran in different circles. I hate to say it, but—and I know how bad it will sound—but . . ."

"Without being too indelicate," his father added, "it was a class situation."

"She . . . I was . . . More and more I was finding her boring," Benton said. "And I'd like to leave it at that."

"Sure," Frank said. "That's fine. No problem at all. How'd y'all meet?"

"I ran into Macy's to grab my little sister a birthday present," he said. "She waited on me. We talked a little. Had an almost instant animal attraction. When I left I had her number. Few days later I called her up and took her out. She . . . it seemed like false advertising. You know the way some girls do. Act like they're up for anything, but then . . . when you get them alone it's a different story. She was way too tame for me."

"Boy's a bit of a bobcat," Benton II said.

"Did you see her on the day she disappeared?"

He shook his head. "Was supposed to. Planned to give her one more chance, then depending on how things went, break up with her at the end of the night. But when I went to pick her up at her shitty apartment, she wasn't home—at least didn't come to the door. That was it. I was done at that point. No more second chances from me."

"Did you go into her apartment?"

He shook his head.

"Had you ever been inside?"

"She was usually out front waiting on me. Think she was embarrassed by the place. Can't blame her. It was a real dump."

"So you've never been inside her apartment?"

"He's not saying that," the attorney sitting closest to him said. "And it doesn't matter. Move on."

"Look, I don't really know anything, okay?" Benton III said.

"Do you know what she did earlier that day?" Frank said.

He shrugged. "Worked, I think. Then went for a run, maybe. She had a smoking hot body. Ran a lot."

"Where did she run?"

"I don't know," he said, as if it was a completely ridiculous question. "Her neighborhood I guess. Sometimes at Stone Mountain I think."

He suddenly glanced over at me.

"That why he's here? Was she taken in Stone Mountain?"

Frank didn't respond.

"That concludes this interview," the one attorney who had spoken said. "We see what you're trying to do now . . . and it's not going to work."

"What is it you think we're trying to do exactly?" Frank said.

"It's obvious," he said. "Set my client up. He had nothing to do with the disappearance of Miss Hepola and doesn't know anything about it. We came in today—voluntarily—to see if we might be able to assist your investigation, but all you're interested in is framing my client because—what?—your investigation has stalled? Well, it's not going to work. Not on my watch."

"I didn't do anything," Benton III said. "I don't have anything to hide."

"Don't say another word, Trey," his dad ordered. "Everyone out. Now."

They all filed out.

As the last and only speaking attorney left, he turned and said, “In the future, direct all questions to me. Not my client. Understood?”

Without waiting for confirmation that it was understood, he turned away again and strolled out behind the others.

“Wonder what the hell that was about?” Frank said when they were gone.

“It was after Stone Mountain came up,” I said. “That’s what they were reacting to.”

He nodded. “Yes it was. And we’re gonna have to find out why.”

13

A few nights later, Susan and I were having a rare dinner out at a little country-style cafe called the Blue Goose, around the corner from our rented farm house in Ellenwood.

The small restaurant, like the food it served, was simple and plain. There was very little in the way of atmosphere or ambiance.

It was early for dinner and only two other tables in the place were occupied—both by elderly couples.

We were here early because we both had to work tonight—she at Scarlett's, me on the sting team at Stone Mountain.

I had come to think of this as possibly our last supper. I wasn't sure we'd still be together after what I wanted to talk to her about.

"What're you gonna have?" she asked, a wry smile on her face.

She knew exactly what I was going to have because I had it every time we ate here. That was my MO. Once I found something I liked at a place, I usually stuck with it.

"I'm not sure," I said. "I'm thinking about the country fried steak with white pepper gravy, green beans, and mashed potatoes."

"Really?" she asked. "Huh. It's just . . . I thought last time we were here you really enjoyed the country fried steak with white pepper gravy, green beans, and mashed potatoes."

"No, I did. You're right. Maybe I should get that again. Just thought I'd try something new."

After we ordered and I started to bring up what I wanted to talk to her about, she began asking me questions about my new job.

"Are you loving it? You're loving it, right?"

I nodded.

"You seem happier in general. How's it goin'? You gettin' settled in okay? Everybody treatin' you right? Y'all any closer to findin' those girls?"

"Yes to everything but finding the missing women," I said.

"I know you've just started but . . . thought any more about changing your major or . . ."

I shrugged. "Not really. Plan to stay in school where I'm at for now. Maybe transfer to Candler when I'm done."

She pursed her lips and nodded.

"How are things with you?" I said. "I feel like I hardly ever see you anymore."

"Same old same for me. Not much changes in my little life."

"Are you happy?"

She shrugged. "I guess. Don't really think about it. Why?"

"I just wondered. I . . . we don't see each other much anymore. I was trying to find out what's going on with you. And the way you said same old same didn't sound . . . very . . ."

"I'm tired most of the time," she said. "And I don't have much time to sit around asking myself how I'm feeling. I just don't. But even if I did, I probably wouldn't."

"You work too much," I said. "I don't want you to be tired all the time or not have enough time to . . . think or—"

"We're barely making it as it is," she said.

"I'm makin' a lot more now," I said. "Or will be very soon. Why don't you quit one of your jobs?"

Wait, what're you doing? You're supposed to be breaking up with her, not making her more dependent on you.

It was true, but I cared about her and felt bad for what seemed to be a joyless life.

She frowned and shook her head. "The truth is, Aunt Margaret can't afford to pay me enough to live on and I can't quit helpin' her, so . . ."

I nodded and thought about it.

"Why?" she asked. "Are you not happy? Is that what this is really about?"

"No, this isn't just about me. I just don't see how you can be happy the way you're living. And if we're not happy . . . we need to make changes so that we—"

"So you're not happy," she said. "But I thought you were now. At least a lot happier than you had been."

"I have much higher job satisfaction," I said. "But that's not exactly the same as being happy, is it?"

"How could you be happier?" she asked.

"Again, I'm not just talking about me," I said.

"Well, let's start with you."

"Okay. For starters . . . I owe you an apology. I've let you do too much."

"I thought . . . I got the feeling from you I didn't do enough."

"I've made it clear I want more time together, more intimacy, more connection, more sex, but I'm talking about the way I've let you . . . mother me . . . enable me. I've let you do too much of . . . that kind of thing. And I want you to stop."

"But I like taking care of you. I'm good at it. I—Are you sayin' I can't do anything for you?"

"Of course not. I do things for you all the time and—that's what a relationship is. But you know the difference. You know what I mean. An act of love or kindness because you want to is very different than . . . doing something out of obligation or because the other person is . . . drinking or . . . being stupid. I'm working on my defects of character and what I'm tellin' you is you've got to let me."

"Okay," she said. "Of course. You know I will. I can do that. I can absolutely do that."

Our food came and our conversation ended and I was filled with an overwhelming sense of futility, like nothing was going to change, like I hadn't adequately communicated what I wanted to, and it wouldn't have done any good if I had.

14

As Erin ran along the sidewalks and trails of Stone Mountain Park, we were stationed in various locations near where she was jogging.

A relatively small operation, the four of us—me, Frank, Walt Thurman, and Joe Ross—moved around to try to keep a visual on Erin as she attempted to attract the attention of a madman.

In her running clothes and with her longish hair worn the way Cheryl Carver had worn hers, Erin looked a lot like the other victims. She was bigger and older but as she ran in the dark it was hard to tell. Like Frank I was apprehensive about this operation, but if someone were going to capture the imagination of the madman, it would be her. This was giving us a good chance at catching him.

The night was cold, and though dim, it wasn't nearly as dark as the first night I had come out here to run.

A waxing crescent moon appeared to hang just above the mountain, drops of moonbeams refracting off the hard, damp, solid granite surface.

"You okay, Erin?" I asked on the radio.

She nodded without saying anything.

"Tol' y'all she was a bad mama jama," Walt said.

She had been jogging on and off—mostly on—for hours. It was truly astounding to see, but I felt like she was overdoing it and wanted her to stop soon.

"You need a break?" I asked.

She shook her head and continued running.

"You're doing great," Frank said. "Just don't overdo it on this first night. He might not even be out here tonight. Pace yourself."

"She's fine," Walt says. "I'm tellin' you she's a—"

"Just a little more tonight," I said. "Just because she can do more doesn't mean she should."

Along with Erin, there were a half dozen other joggers in the park, a few middle-aged female walkers, and at least two couples pushing a jogging stroller.

Earlier there were far more people present.

"Look at them," Walt said over the radio. "Given what we know . . . they look so . . . exposed, like a damn herd of unsuspecting wildebeests or somethin'."

"You been watchin' some nature shit on public television again?" Joe asked.

"Hey, man, what I do in the privacy of my own home is my business."

While Walt and Joe went up the mountain walking path ahead of Erin, Frank and I stayed at the base to keep Erin between us.

"We'll call it after this," Frank said.

I nodded. "Think we need to."

"You settling in okay?" he asked.

"Yeah. Great little department. You were right about Bud. He's a . . . He's very surprising. Very refreshing."

He nodded, then looked around. "Where do you think the women are? Out here somewhere?"

"I have no idea," I said. "Absolutely none. But . . . I went to a couple of the road schools with a psychologist who lives here."

"Here—Stone Mountain? Or here—Atlanta?"

"Atlanta," I said. "She's studied and consulted with the FBI's Behavioral Unit. She's working on becoming a profiler. She's not official or anything. Hasn't had any actual firsthand training. But she's good. If she's willing . . . I'd like to get her take on what we're dealing with here. She wouldn't say anything to anybody and I think she'd have a lot to contribute."

"We need all the help we can get," he said. "Just keep her out of the way—and out of the view of the press—and let her know if she talks to anyone at all she'll be jeopardizing any future she might have in profiling."

"Thanks and I will, but it won't be an issue. She keeps clients' secrets all the time. She's a true pro."

He nodded to me, then said into the radio, "Let's call it a night."

Erin broke radio silence for the first time. "I can do more, Frank. He probably doesn't attack until late at night anyway."

"I know, and I appreciate it," he said. "I appreciate all you've done and I know how bad you want to get him. We all do, but we'll be back tomorrow night. This is probably gonna take a while, so we better all pace ourselves and—"

"Truth is," Joe Ross said, "we don't even know for sure that he's snatching 'em here."

"That's true, but—"

And then another voice came across the radio—one from the forensic search team—and just like that we knew for sure.

"Frank, it's Gerald. We found something. And it's bad."

15

While still watching her, we let Erin walk to her car alone —not wanting to break her cover in case she was being watched.

We then drove west around Robert E. Lee Boulevard to a wooded area about halfway between the entrance of the walkup trail and the famous north face where the laser light show took place.

Parking on the side of the road behind one of the search team vans, we entered the woods, crossed over the railroad tracks and continued toward the base of the mountain.

Eventually, we arrived at crime scene tape stretched around the bases of pine trees and a portable bank of lights trained down on what looked to be the badly broken body of a naked young woman.

Gerald Manning was a short, roundish, middle-aged man with a puffy red face, large glasses, and bushy strawberry-blond mustache. What little there was of his hair was grown out in long, thin strands that swooped across the top of his head.

I didn't know what his title was or exactly what he did and I didn't ask.

As we approached, he spoke directly to Frank, who didn't bother with introducing us.

"If she weren't nude . . ." Gerald began, "and other things hadn't been done to her body . . . I'd've said it was possible that she slipped and fell or maybe even jumped, but . . ."

The granite rock mountain loomed above us in the dimness, an incomprehensible dark mass felt more than seen.

"Any idea who she is yet?" Frank asked.

Gerald shook his head. "Lot we can't tell because of the damage from the impact and the deterioration of the body. She's been out here a while. Even in the cold weather we've been having . . . decomposition's pretty bad. We got skin slippage and though the bugs have started on her, no critters or wildlife have yet. Probably found her just before that started."

Before we got close enough to really see the body I had wondered if it was even one of our missing women, but once I could see her, I knew it was. Her hair and build, her age and body type confirmed it—even in the mangled condition it was in.

She was facedown, which was a grace, but mostly the body looked like a crumpled bag of bones, as if the skeleton inside the mound of skin and hair wasn't attached. One arm was out, as if flung back at an odd angle.

I broke out in a cold, clammy sweat as my throat constricted and my stomach seemed to bottom out.

I could feel myself getting sick and I had to look away a minute, swallow hard, and take several deep breaths.

Joe said, "Don't suicides sometimes take their clothes off before jumping? Could this just be a—"

He and Frank and I were the only ones to arrive so far.

"She was murdered," Gerald said to Frank as if he had been the one who asked the question.

"Are you sure?" Joe said. "Isn't that her wrist? Looks like she cut it."

Again he only looked at and spoke to Frank. "She was cut on

some—including her wrists—but she didn't do it herself. Her wrists and ankles were bound. The one that's visible there slipped out of the binding as it decomposed or maybe because of the impact. There's gonna be a limit to what we can tell until we do an autopsy—and even then . . . the body's in such bad shape . . . there's a lot we just won't be able to tell—but from what I've been able to observe so far, I'd say she was cut on some by a very big, very sharp knife, but not a whole lot and none of those wounds were fatal. I think she was alive when her killer flung her off the mountain."

Walt and Erin, who had gone by the inn for Erin to change, walked up and joined us.

"Oh my God," Erin said. "Is . . ."

"She one of the ones we lookin' for?" Walt asked.

Frank nodded. "Think so."

"We'll know more once we get her back and do an autopsy," Gerald said, "but our best bet is gonna be to find a more recent victim who hasn't been as exposed to the elements as long, hasn't decomposed as much."

"Kathy Dady," Erin whispered. "We need to find Kathy Dady."

We all nodded.

"We think there are at least three more out here," Frank said. "One of them has only been missing four days."

"We need to increase our search teams," Gerald said, "but if he killed them all the same way, we at least know where to look. 'Course the base of the mountain is five miles around and some of it's very treacherous terrain. But . . . who knows . . . maybe we'll get lucky."

"Good work, Gerald," Frank said. "Thank you."

"I'll call you when I've got the prelim—or we find another one."

Frank began backing out and walking toward our vehicles.

We all followed.

We walked along in silence for a while, each of us seeming

overwhelmed with the brutality and enormity of what we had just seen.

"That was so stupid," Frank said.

"What was?" Joe asked.

Frank glanced over at Erin. "Havin' you out here tonight like bait when we didn't know what we were dealing with. This isn't amateur hour. I know better than that. Had no idea . . . killer like this . . . you don't do a half-assed sting operation . . . Don't toss out some bait on a string. I could've gotten you killed tonight. I'm sorry."

"I was honored to do it," Erin said. "I'm happy to keep doin' it. Planned on it. More so now after seeing what we just saw. No need to apologize to me. To me that just confirmed we're doing the right thing."

16

Four very long days later, Erin, Walt, Joe, and I were eating lunch at a hamburger joint in the little town of Stone Mountain when Daphne Littleton, a TV reporter with WSB, showed up.

A lot had happened over the past few days.

The other three missing young women's bodies were found, we had chased down leads and searched for connections, and witnessed as word was spreading over the metro area about what was happening out here in Stone Mountain.

We were all eating light because of a meeting with the medical examiner we had later that afternoon.

Joe was saying how unfair it was that I didn't have to wear a uniform when I saw the WSB van pull into the parking lot.

I thought again how grateful I was not to have to wear the uniform for now—particularly the turtleneck, which had always made me feel like I was being choked.

"It's just temporary," Erin said. "Soon as this case is over and the task force is disbanded he'll be—"

"You're the one who needs to be in plainclothes," Walt said to her. "If there's even a chance we're gonna run the sting operation again."

"That's true," I said.

"Probably shouldn't be seen with you losers either," she said.

I had enjoyed getting to know and work with these guys, and though they were all between five and ten years older than I was, I felt accepted by and a certain camaraderie with them.

I was learning their why—why they did this job, what had first drawn them to it—and was growing to respect and appreciate them. Erin's younger sister had been killed by a drunk driver when she was a teenager, and though she didn't actually come out and say it, I gathered from what she'd said that she too had been a victim of violent crime. My guess was a sexual assault. Joe's stepdad had been a security guard most of his life. Walt's older brother had gotten in a gang when he was young and had been killed in a drive-by, and him being a cop was the culmination of his choosing away from the path his brother had taken.

We didn't have much in common and wouldn't have hung out together otherwise, but a bond was forming and I was enjoying both the belonging and sobriety I was experiencing.

"I think we should all be plainclothes as long as we're on the task force," Joe said.

"Then talk to Bud," Walt said. "Not us."

"Think I will."

"And your white ass best not show up wearing a rebel flag t-shirt or some shit like that," Walt said, smiling to expose more of the spaces between his small teeth. "What the hell kind of plain clothes you got anyway? Flannel and camouflage?"

"What's wrong with that?" Joe said. "Whatta you got? Some Michael Jackson sequined pants and one glove shit?"

"Oh, 'cause I'm black. I get it," Walt said, his deep voice rich with sarcasm. "Good one."

When Daphne came in, she walked directly over to me.

"Hey John," she said.

I stood and spoke to her, hoping she'd leave it at that and move along.

"Mind if I join you guys?" she said.

"We were just about to leave," I said. "We have a meeting to get back to."

"Is it about the serial killer?" she asked. "I hear Stone Mountain has a serial killer. Just like in the movies."

Daphne had dyed blond hair and wore too much makeup. She had a great, natural body and was fairly attractive—though she looked better on camera than in person. A good bit older than me, she had often been flirtatious or actually somewhat sexually aggressive with me, and I wondered if it was just her way of being in the world.

"We can't comment on an ongoing investigation," I said. "You know that."

"Off the record," she said. "Just background for—"

"There's no such thing," Erin said, her voice flat and stern. "Would you excuse us please? We need to finish our lunch and get back to work."

It was interesting to see the two women juxtaposed the way they were. They both wore too much makeup, but couldn't have been more different. One had TV looks, the other the plainness you'd expect in a uniformed female cop, but whereas there was something decidedly fake about Daphne, even in her plainness and unflattering uniform, Erin was the more authentically attractive of the two.

"Sure, okay," she said. "John, my number's the same. Use it. You owe me and if this is what I think it is, it's what I want to cash in my marker on. And don't forget . . . I can help y'all. Just let me know what message you need to get out there and—"

"Have a nice day," Erin said without meaning it.

Daphne nodded without seeming offended and left.

"How do you know her?" Walt said. "She's . . . sexy as . . ."

"Yeah," Joe said, "I got something she can report on."

"What," Walt said, "an investigative series on limp dicks?"

Joe's pale, thin face flushed with embarrassment and anger, and his narrowed eyes seemed to turn black.

It wasn't the first time Walt had alluded to Joe's impotence—something that seemed to be common knowledge at the station—but I had never seen Joe react with such anger or embarrassment, and I tried to change the subject.

"She covered the LaMarcus Williams and Cedric Porter cases," I said. "I helped Frank some with them."

"I heard you did more than help," Erin said, and I could tell from her awkward glances that she was trying to change the subject off of Joe's impotence too.

"How'd you and Frank become such pals?" Walt asked.

"Family friend. He and my dad are . . . have worked on some cases together."

An awkward silence followed, during which everyone either ate another bite or took a sip of their soda. Eventually, Joe seemed to calm down some.

"Your dad's a cop too?" Joe asked.

I nodded. "Sheriff in Florida. Helped some with the Ted Bundy case."

"Just remember," Walt said. "You's a private citizen when you helped out on them other cases. You're a cop now. No media. No exceptions."

I shook my head. "I won't say anything to anybody," I said.

"Nobody sayin' you can't get freaky with her," he said, "just use your mouth for other things 'sides talkin'. Make her think you're gonna give her some info if she gives you some . . . then be all like psyche."

I shook my head again. "Not interested," I said. "She's not—"

"You sayin' she's fair game? 'Cause I will use that little maneuver on her fine ass, I kid you not."

Erin shook her head. "It's not worth it. Stay as far away from her and others like her as you can. You can thank me later."

"You serious?" he said. "Weren't you and ol' redneck Joe here tryin' to get me out of my uniform before she walked up?"

"Actually, that was just Joe, but while we're on the subject, I wasn't saying don't get with another cop," she said. "Not at all. I'll bring the cuffs and you bring the nightstick."

"Fuck that," he said. "I saw how long you ran the other night. Couldn't keep up with you. 'Sides . . . not exactly sure what you got in mind with a damn nightstick."

"It'd be worth getting in shape for," she said. "I kid you not. And if you don't want me using the nightstick on you just say so."

"I don't want you using the nightstick on me," he said.

"Hey, I'm already in pretty good shape," Joe said. "Just sayin' . . ."

"You're not in as good shape as you think you are," she said.

"Skinny don't equal strength or endurance, white boy," Walt said.

I was mildly amused by their banter, but it also gave me a strong sense of trepidation.

We were a small group of inexperienced, immature young people playing at being cops. We were no match for the madman throwing the bodies of young women off the side of the mountain.

When I went to the restroom a short while later, Daphne Littleton was waiting on me.

"I meant what I said, John. I want this one. Bad. And you owe me. You told me you'd pay me back someday. Well, today is that day."

She was one of the most openly ambitious people I had ever encountered. It was raw and exposed and though I found it indecent and embarrassing, there was a certain honesty and integrity to it.

"You shouldn't be in here," I said. "You shouldn't have come here like this—done this in front of my colleagues."

"Sorry, I didn't think that part through, but . . . doesn't change anything."

"It does for me. I would have worked with you to the extent I could. I would have given you what I could have that didn't jeopardize the investigation, but now—because you've called me out in front of everyone—I can't give you anything."

"You need to think about this, John. It's not just that you owe me. It's not just that I can help you. I can hurt you. You don't want me as an enemy."

"You need to think more long-term," I said. "We'll be able to help each other in the future. Don't set fire to all the bridges just yet. Walt Thurman, another officer in our department, just expressed interest in helping you."

"He's just horny."

"You sayin' you can't make that work?"

"Hasn't worked with you so far," she said. "Still say we could be awfully damn good together. I know I'm a little older than you, but . . ."

My guess was that she was in her early thirties—over a decade older than me.

". . . that's okay," she said. "I could teach you things."

"I'm sure you could," I said, "but I'm with someone."

"So? I'm not proposing marriage, just some fun. You ever have any of that?"

"Yes," I said. "With my girlfriend."

"Okay," she said. "But think about it. For now . . . give me whatshisname's number and don't forget you still owe me. Big time. I'll take a kiss and a confirmation we've got a serial killer, too."

17

"I asked Gerald to come give us a summary of what we know so far," Frank said. "The more we know from the outset the better our investigation will be and the quicker we'll catch the guy doing this. Please take notes. We need to all be on the same page for this."

Bud had welcomed everyone to his department then turned it over to Frank.

In addition to everyone we had before, we were joined by a couple of other GBI agents, Bobby Meredith and an additional Stone Mountain Park cop, and two sheriff's investigators from the counties where two of the victims were from.

Our group was growing, as I knew it would, and as word spread about what we were dealing with, it would only get worse.

We were packed into the too-small conference room—some of us at the table, others at seats along the wall, others standing, at least two guys mostly out in the hallway, their heads hovering in the doorway.

"This is all very preliminary," Gerald said. "But like Frank said, the more you can know now, the better. We'll give you updates as we can. There's things I can't tell you because we just don't know yet, but what I do tell you today are things we know to be true. Okay?"

Several of us nodded.

"Okay, so . . . we've found four victims so far," he said, "and we've identified them as four missing young women from the metro area. There could be other victims—ones we don't know about because they weren't reported missing or . . . who knows, so we have a team continuing to search the park."

Frank cleared his throat and said, "We've identified the bodies of Cheryl Carver, Paula Nichols, Shelly Hepola, and Kathy Dady. We believe all four women were abducted while jogging in Stone Mountain Park."

"Yes," Gerald said. "Each victim was—"

"Let me—sorry to interrupt again, Gerald," Frank said, "but let me say just a few things more first. Okay?"

"Of course."

"I know I keep saying this," Frank said, "but I'm gonna keep on saying it. Not a word of this leaves this room. Don't talk to reporters. Don't talk to your friends. Don't even talk to your mama about this. Understand?"

Everyone nodded.

"I mean it. If you talk, you're not just off the task force, you'll be brought up on disciplinary charges and could even lose your job. It's that serious. Now . . . I know some aspects of this are new to some of us. This is a rare and strange thing we're dealing with here. Some of you may have worked the Atlanta Child Murders a few years back, but this isn't something we get every day. What we're dealing with is a serial killer. This particular kind of killer has certain patterns and predictable behaviors. He commits a series of murders, usually with a similar type of victim, but unlike a mass murder—like James Huberty at the San Diego McDonald's—the serial killer's murders are more spread out with time in between, known as a cooling-off period. And unlike most other murders, a serial killer often kills strangers, chosen for some motive that is not obvious to us. Okay, Gerald, I won't interrupt again."

"No, it's good," Gerald said. "Good foundational stuff. Okay, so what we have here in this case are four victims so far—all joggers jogging around Stone Mountain when they were abducted. They're all around the same age range—eighteen to twenty-six—all have a similar build and look—thin, athletic, long straight hair, sort of what you might call plain-looking girls. Athletes."

"There's something about them—the way they look, act, move, speak, run, walk, play with their hair—something that draws him to them," Frank said. "They are his type. It's the only reason they're part of his series."

"Each victim was dropped from the mountain," Gerald said. "They were all alive when they went off the mountain, and though they each had a few small cuts from a knife, it was the fall and impact that killed them."

"Fuck," Walt said.

"Yeah," Joe added. "Can you imagine the terror of being pushed off a mountain and falling to your death?"

"Can you girls hold it down?" one of the sheriff's investigators said. "I'm trying to hear what the man has to say so we can catch this prick."

"I gotcha prick," Walt said.

"Your girls, too," Joe added.

Ignoring them, Gerald continued. "All the victims were bound at the ankles and wrists and the wrist bindings are part of a long lead rope, as if he pulled them around—perhaps walking them up the mountain or something like that. Two were found on the ground and two were caught in tree branches. They were all nude."

"Have we recovered any of their clothes or belongings so far?" Frank asked.

Gerald shook his head. "Nothing. Not a shred from any of them."

I thought about what Summer had said about two of the girls not being grounded or touching the ground. As usual she had been right. She had an incredible gift.

"A serial killer often keeps a memento from his victims," Frank said. "A trophy from his kill or more likely an item that reminds him of the kill so he can relive it over and over and fuel his fantasies with it. Maybe he's keeping all their belongings as part of that."

"What about their vehicles?" Erin asked. "If they were abandoned in the park, why weren't we notified? Why didn't four abandoned vehicles raise an alarm for—"

"None of them were left in the park," Gerald said. "The killer must have moved them after he killed the young women. They were found all over the metro area. In fact, the searches for these missing persons have been centered around the areas where their cars were found."

"There is no sign of sexual assault on any of the victims," Gerald said.

"I thought serial killers were sexually motivated?" one of the GBI agents said.

"Not always, no," Gerald said. "Of course, the crimes can be sexually motivated without the killer having sex with the victims, but no, not all serial killers are sexually motivated."

"Interesting," he said. "Learn something new every day."

"All of the victims were killed around the time they were abducted," Gerald said. "I mean within a matter of hours. He doesn't keep them long. Long enough to perform his rituals with them—whatever all he's doing, we don't know yet—and to get them up the mountain and do whatever he does up there with them. Again, we're talking hours not days."

"Wonder what he is doing if he's not raping them," Walt said.

"I look forward to asking him," Frank said.

"One of the things he's doing," Gerald said, "is washing them. He's bathing them and washing their hair before making them plunge to their death."

"Any sign they were drugged?" Bud asked.

"Toxicology's gonna take a while, so . . . don't have an answer to that one yet."

"Any physical evidence been found?" I asked. "Footprints? Fingerprints? Hair? Fibers?"

He shook his head. "Nothing. The bodies have all been cleaned, the hair washed. So they've not yielded up any trace evidence of any kind. As far as footprints or . . . We don't know exactly where he dropped them from—just that it was a different place each time. But even if we did, it's doubtful we'd find any prints. The granite itself wouldn't hold a print, so it'd have to be one of the few areas of indentation where dirt has collected, but then how would we know it was the killer's and not a tourist's? As far as where the bodies were found . . . there's no evidence that the killer visited those areas. Haven't found anything to suggest anyone has."

Frank said, "We've had teams searching the mountain—both the top as well as around the base and the park police are helping us with a thorough search of the park."

At that Bobby Meredith, the large, goofy park police liaison, half stood and gave a little wave.

"We're nowhere near done with the park," Frank continued. "Gonna take a while. But so far we haven't turned up anything."

There were a few nods, but no one spoke.

"Anything else before we let you go?" Frank asked.

Gerald seemed to think about it. "Ah, yes. Just one thing. Even though the killer washes the bodies, they smell of smoke and at least two of the young women had char marks or soot on their skin, so he's keeping them close to a fire or . . . somehow fire or ash is involved."

I immediately began thinking what I bet everyone else was

thinking at that moment—Stone Mountain Park has the largest campground in the state. There was a good chance the killer was camping in the park or at least using a campsite to do what he was doing to them.

18

"We've got to move fast on this thing," Frank said. "Word's going to get out and then it'll be a circus. Reporters. Other cops wanting in. Armchair detectives. Psychics. We'll lose all control."

When Gerald left, several of the other cops did too, including the other GBI agents and the two Stone Mountain Park police.

We were back to our core group.

Bud noted and reiterated what Frank had just said, adding, "We have hours, not days before there'll be a very bright light pointed directly at us."

The two middle-aged men made an interesting pair. Though roughly the same age, though roughly in the same profession, they appeared to be from different eras. Bud, with his black trousers, white shirt, black tie and shoes, gray crewcut and big black horn-rimmed glasses, looked like a 60s era G-man. Frank, with his navy blue pants, light blue Oxford button-down, too wide red tie, military style haircut, and brown semi-casual dress shoes looked like a conservative politician serving in a southern state house or a girls basketball coach at a junior college.

"We're gonna need some additional help for the legwork," Frank said. "I can get a few more GBI agents, but we'll have to use some of the other agencies too. We need people at every funeral, visitation, and graveside service. We need someone working with a family member or close friend to identify anyone who doesn't belong. We need a photographer taking pictures."

He paused, but by the time I had looked up from the notes I was taking, he had started again.

"We'll need more help with the door-to-door where the victims lived—see if any neighbors saw anyone hanging around or anything out of the ordinary. We need to beef up patrol in the park. We need to—"

"They're not going to close the park?" Erin asked.

He shook his head. "The best we could get them to do is include a warning in our statement to the media."

"Oh my God," she said.

"Said if we catch this guy quickly, it won't be a problem."

"Then that's what we need to damn well do," Joe said.

"We've got to beef up security and patrol," Frank said, "but we need to be investigating too. We need to gather information about everyone who we know has been in the park during this time. There won't be a record of most visitors, but anyone who had to register—in the inn or campground—anyone who paid with a credit card. We need to go through all the souvenir pictures that've been taken. We need to interview every worker, every hotel guest, every camper."

"I was thinkin'," Joe said.

"God help us all," Walt said.

"The char mark and smoke smell on the victims . . . I'm thinkin' our guy's a camper."

Frank nodded. "Or is using a campsite. It's definitely where we have to start."

"I think I should go undercover," he said.

"How's that?" Bud said.

"I think I should camp in the park," Joe said. "I've got all the equipment. I know how to camp. I could keep an eye on things, investigate without anyone there knowing I was."

Frank looked at Bud. Bud was already nodding.

"I like that idea," Frank said.

"Me too," Bud added. "Good thinking, Joe. We'll still need you doing other duties during the day, but . . . if you're willing to camp there for the next few days . . . that'd be great."

"Happy to do it," he said.

"I think we need to do that and continue with the sting operation," Erin said. "Things like that are our best chance of catching him. We've got to be active and move fast. And don't you dare tell me it's okay for Joe to be out there in harm's way but not me."

"It's different," Bud said. "Joe isn't out there as bait. He's not the killer's type."

"He ain't nobody's type," Walt said, smiling his big small tooth smile. "'Cept maybe one of his barefoot cousins."

"Okay," she said. "It's cool. I get it."

"I'm not saying no," Bud said, "just . . ."

"Here's somethin' for y'all to think about," Walt said. "If y'all don't do the sting operation . . . she's just gonna go out there by herself on her own time and run, so . . . it'd be better to have us out there with her."

"That true?" Frank asked her.

She smiled. "I'd rather not discuss what I do on my own time. It's personal and private."

"Okay, Uncle," Bud said. "We can do it, but only on select times and with plenty of support team cover. I don't want to have to put up a memorial to one of my officers in the squad room. Understand?"

"Yes, sir," she said, as the others nodded.

"The yes, sir is a nice touch," he said. "Especially as you're forcing me to do what you want."

"Okay," Frank said. "I'll split up the tasks and do some

recruiting and create teams assigned to each task. Here's what we can start with right now."

19

That evening I ran into Summer Grantham at the Stone Mountain Inn.

"We were right," she said, frowning.

As if her uniform, she was dressed in a classic rock tee, blue jeans, and Keds sneakers. Like her shoes, the blue Stones t-shirt had a British flag on it. Her blond hair was in a ponytail, and her pale roundish face looked far younger than she really was. In fact, everything about her was cute and youthful.

"What're you doing here?" I asked.

"I work here," she said. "I'm one of the night managers. My shift starts in a few hours. You got time to sit a minute?"

"Sure," I said.

She led me out of the back of the hotel lobby and into the courtyard where we sat on a bench not far from the pool.

"Why are you at work a few hours early?" I asked.

She shrugged. "Nothing better to do," she said. "Trying to stay close to the . . . action. See if I can pick up anything. I don't know. Is it true y'all've found four victims so far?"

I nodded. It was information that would be going out in the press release tomorrow anyway.

"There are more," she said. "I hope y'all are still looking. I'm not sure there are more here—in the park—but he has more victims."

I nodded. "Thank you."

"We've got to stop him," she said. "He's not gonna stop if we don't."

The backdoor of the lobby swung open and a young black man stuck his head out. "Summer, get in here. You've got to see this. We've got a serial killer here at Stone Mountain. An honest-to-God serial killer."

We ran into the lobby and joined a small group of staff and guests gathered around the TV.

Daphne Littleton was in the foreground of the shot, the north face of the mountain in the background behind her.

". . . an active serial killer situation," she was saying. "Some in law enforcement have dubbed him the Stone Cold Killer because of his method of murder. He's actually using the mountain itself as a weapon, plunging the poor victims to their terrifying deaths. Four so far. Again this is a WSB exclusive. I'm Daphne Littleton."

I shook my head as the people in the small group around me gasped and reacted to the report.

As soon as the report ended, my radio began to go off. It was Bud summoning us to his office.

"What the hell?" Bud said.

"Ask him," Walt said, nodding toward me.

"Why him?" Frank said.

"She's his buddy. He owed her a story from some previous deal they worked on together."

I was shocked at what Walt was doing, but I shouldn't have been. Instantly self-conscious and defensive, I could feel my heart rate rising as the sting of embarrassment spreading across my face.

"She the one who helped on the Cedric Porter case?" Frank asked.

I nodded.

"Did you give her the story?" Bud asked.

I shook my head. "She came in where we were eating lunch today and told me she'd heard something about the case and reminded me that I owed her," I said. "Everyone here heard what I said. Then when I went to the restroom later she was in there waiting for me. Said the same stuff. I told her I couldn't give her anything and I didn't. Whoever she got all that from, it wasn't me."

"Y'all were in the bathroom together and she has all this inside information," Walt said, "and you didn't give it to her."

"Did you tell anyone about it?" Bud asked. "At least let Frank know she was—"

I shook my head. "I was going to, but haven't had a chance yet. Everyone saw her approach me—"

"Not in the damn bathroom we didn't," Walt said.

"How long has it been since lunch?" I asked. "Six hours? More? You think I gave her all that info at lunch and she just sat on it for over six hours?"

"She could've been verifying it," Walt said. "Or waiting for the evening news."

I thought about her asking for Walt's number, and though I didn't give it to her—I only had the station number, which she already had—I wondered if she had spoken to him. Or more importantly if he had spoken to her.

I shook my head. "She wouldn't have waited and even if they did wait for the evening news, it would have been the top story at five. She got this info this evening—after our meeting this afternoon. She got it from somebody in there, but it wasn't me."

"I hope not," Bud said. "I hope she didn't get it from any of us."

"She didn't," Joe said.

Erin nodded. "None of us would give her anything and I don't believe John did."

"I know the two GBI agents didn't," Frank said.

"That leaves the park PD guys and the sheriff's investigators."

"Well, whoever it was," Frank said. "It's out now and we've got to deal with it."

20

"The hell was that about?" I asked.

I had caught up to Walt as we were walking out of the building. The only other person around was Erin and she was up ahead of us.

"Whatcha mean?" he said.

"I didn't talk to the reporter," I said. "But if you thought I did, why not come to me? Ask me about it first?"

"You damn sure did talk to that reporter," he said. "Twice."

Erin slowed her pace to let us catch up to her.

"I meant I didn't tell her anything about the case."

"All I know is what we all saw and that's all I said in there."

"But . . . why not ask me first? Why not give me—"

"I don't know you," he said. "I don't owe you anything. Far as I'm concerned you're a punk ass kid who shouldn't be involved in any of this."

Erin moved over in between us. "Walt, that's enough."

"I'm serious. You actin' like I should know you wouldn't give info to the press. But I don't know that. I don't know you. We just started working together. It's not personal. Don't take it personally. But think about it. We see you talkin' to a reporter at lunch and she says you owe her, then that evening she's reporting about our case on the news . . . what the hell am I supposed to think? Tell me that. My job means something to me. I'm not gonna do anything to jeopardize it. If you're straight you'll be down with that. You'll get it. If you're not, well, fuck you."

"Okay," I said, "If I take you at your word—something you're not willing to do for me—then I get where you're coming from and I appreciate it. I didn't tell Daphne Littleton anything about our case. Not a word. And I wouldn't. This case means more to me than . . . It's not just a job to me. And the truth is, I feel the same way about the person who did as you do me. So I get it."

"Whatcha mean if you take me at my word?" he said. "How else could you take it?"

"Seriously?" I asked. "Like you're the one who talked to her—like you said you were going to—and now you're trying to cover your tracks by blaming me."

"Walt's a good man," Erin was saying. "An honest cop."

We were standing outside the station in the cool darkness, the traffic moving through the little downtown area thinner and slower and more intermittent now.

Walt had just left. I was still angry and frustrated and embarrassed.

I had lingered hoping to talk to Erin about it.

"He's concerned about his job, but he's concerned about the case too. That was his version of doing the right thing. He doesn't trust easily. You're the new guy and we did all see you talking to the reporter, who seemed to know you quite well and did say you owed her. He'll cool down and over time he'll start to trust you. But it will be slow. It's just the way he is."

I nodded. "Thanks."

"I know he made the joke about gettin' with her, but . . . that was just talk," she said. "He didn't mean anything by it. He's got a girlfriend he adores. He'd never do anything to jeopardize that. It's just his way. Just . . . bravado."

I nodded again. "I honestly didn't tell her anything," I said.

She nodded. "It'll come out who did," she said. "Almost always does."

21

I met Ernestine Campbell at Scarlett's, and I had an ulterior motive for doing so.

Ernie was a middle-aged black woman with an athletic build, especially for her age. She had a background in psychology and for the past decade had been applying it to forensics.

I had met her at some of the road school training sessions the FBI had put on for area law enforcement agencies and we had connected over the Atlanta Child Murders case.

I had asked her to meet me here because, like Margaret, her partner had died recently and she was single.

"I saw the news segment on two," she said. "No controlling this thing now."

I nodded and frowned. "We didn't even get a full day with the details."

"Which are what exactly?"

"Four young women abducted while jogging at Stone Mountain," I said. "All killed near the time of their abduction. All with small cuts. All naked. All washed. All bound at the wrists and ankles. All smelling of smoke and at least two with charred marks on their skin. All killed by being thrown off the mountain."

"And they're all similar?"

I nodded again. "All young, athletic . . . longish light brown or dark blond hair. All pretty but plain—and I guess more attractive than pretty. Wore little to no makeup. Seemed to be sort of loners."

Susan arrived with our drinks—coffee for me, a glass of chardonnay for Ernie.

"Thank you," I said. "How's your day going?"

"It's okay. Long. I'm tired, but . . ."

"Where's Margaret?"

"She's already gone. Why?"

"Was gonna introduce her to Ernie."

"Why?" Ernie asked. "She a single lesbian too?"

I smiled.

"He means well," Susan said.

"It's sweet," Ernie said.

"Margaret, my aunt, is an alcoholic. She's barely surviving. I wouldn't wish her on anyone right now."

"I thought dating a beautiful, together, psychologist would be just what she needed," I said.

Susan looked at me and narrowed her eyes. "And what would Miss Ernestine get out of it?"

I shrugged. "Free drinks? Carnal pleasure? I don't know."

"Bless your heart," Ernie said. "Such a sweet boy."

"Sweet and slow," Susan said, and moved away.

"How are things between you two?" Ernie asked.

I frowned. "Not great."

She nodded knowingly. "A relationship hasn't fixed your issues, has it? Why would you think it would Margaret's?"

"That's just the special kind of fool I am, I guess."

"Go visit with your young lady for a few minutes and let me look over the case file, then come back and we'll talk it through."

"The Stone Cold Killer, huh?" Susan said. "Bet you anything Daphne gave him that name herself."

"You sure you're up for this . . . after . . ."

I was leaning over my side of the bar and she was leaning over hers. Meeting in the middle, we were speaking quietly so that the handful of regulars around the bar couldn't hear us. The jukebox was playing so I was pretty sure our conversation was private.

I nodded. "Happiest I've been in a while."

"Oh, that's what a girl wants to hear."

"You know what I meant," I said.

"I think you said exactly what you meant," she said.

"I didn't come over here to argue with you," I said. "But it seems like that's all we do these days."

She shook her head. "That's a *glass-half-empty* take on the situation. We're just both tired and stressed and don't get enough time together."

"Speaking of . . ." I said. "How late you working?"

"I told you," she said. "Margaret's already gone. I've got to close. It'll be late."

"Then I guess I'll go back out to Stone Mountain when I leave here," I said. "We could've just met out there, but I wanted to see you—at least for a few minutes."

"And try to setup Ernie and Margaret. Don't forget that. Though . . . if you're so unhappy in our relationship why would you wish one on anyone else?"

"I'll need more time," Ernie said. "And more info as it comes in . . . to do an actual profile, but . . . there's the basic, obvious stuff. He's a white male. Most of these type killers tend to hunt within their own race. Probably between eighteen and thirty-five. Most are. He's nocturnal—most of what he's doing is at night. He's strong, athletic, probably a runner himself, but definitely in shape. He's patient and careful. I'd say he's on the mid-to-upper end of the age range and he probably holds down a job —nothing too demanding but he functions just fine in society behind his mask of sanity. If the typical pattern holds, he's probably applied for a law enforcement job or will at the very least try to help with the investigation in some way—especially now that it's so public. Pay close attention to your tip line calls or eye witnesses. He'll probably be at more than one crime scene or area of interest and will be anxious to explain why he is. Obviously the mountain has significance to him and the things he's doing with the victims are ritualistic, but . . . the manner of murder is . . . cold, impersonal. He's got a knife, but he doesn't kill them with it, just cuts on them a very small amount. Stabbing them or cutting them to death and then throwing them off the mountain would be far more fulfilling to a certain type of sadist. We're gonna have to think about why he's doing what he's doing. What need does it meet in him? What purpose does it serve in his narrative? I'd say he's above average intelligence . . . and experienced . . . It's taken a lot to get him to where he is now—many other acts, crimes, experimentation. It's interesting that there's no sign of sexual assault. I'd say these are sexually motivated crimes, but—"

"What if he's washing them because he's ejaculating on them instead of in them?" I asked.

She nodded. "That would fit. He's not penetrating them—for whatever reason—but he's using them sexually, then cleaning them. That would explain why he's washing them. Typically that's something done after death as part of the staging or displaying his work. But in this case he does it while they're still alive. No evidence that he even goes to the bodies after they're dead, let alone does anything to them."

"Wonder if the cuts on them are from when he's sexually assaulting them," I said. "Maybe he's holding the knife on them and it moves some as he's masturbating or . . . maybe it symbolizes the penetration. His blade penetrates their bodies because he can't."

She nodded. "I like that. Remember what the FBI instructors said about the difference between MO and signature?"

I nodded.

MO or *modus operandi* is fluid and flexible, a learned behavior, but the killer's psychological signature is fixed, often subconscious. Even if it was pointed out to him, even if he tried not to, he'd still leave it.

"We need to figure out which is which," she said. "The truth is . . . we need more information to be able to come up with much more. And of course . . . the only way we're gonna get more information is if he kills again, which we hope he doesn't."

"No way he doesn't," I said.

"But . . . it'll be interesting to see if with all the attention and media coverage and knowing y'all are watching the mountain if he'll keep doing it there, keep doing it the same way. If so, and if he can get away with it . . . it'd be an extraordinary feat. But if he changes his MO then we'll get a better look at his true signature."

22

"Sorry I had to leave so abruptly earlier," I said.

"Don't be," Summer said. "It's no problem. That was a big development."

She was wearing her uniform and standing behind the desk in the lobby of the Stone Mountain Inn. At the moment we were the only two people around."

"I can't believe they're not closing the park," she said.

"Really? You can't believe they'd put profit ahead of people?"

"Well, yeah, you're right, but . . . I did notice there are more police patrolling the park."

I nodded slowly and frowned. "Chances are he'll just see that as a bigger challenge."

"You don't think he'll stop or move somewhere else to do it?"

"Not on your life," I said.

"I really don't understand this at all," she said. "I can sense the darkness, but the workings of the mind of the man are a complete mystery to me."

"That's a good thing," I said.

"I guess it is," she said. "I just . . . want to be more help. Speaking of . . . is there any way I can help you? I mean other than the guest list you asked for. I was thinking . . . I have a room here. I'm actually living here at the moment. Obviously, I don't use it at night . . . so if you ever want to stay out here . . . you're welcome to. There are actually two beds—just consider one of them yours."

"Thank you, Summer," I said. "I really appreciate that. And will probably take you up on it."

"I wish you would. Anytime."

Summer was enigmatic and difficult to read, so I couldn't tell if she were just offering a place for me to sleep or something more. We had been involved briefly about a year ago, but I had broken it off after too many times of her vanishing without a word for days at a time. Also, a reporter had told me that in a few of the cases she had assisted with she had actually become a suspect.

"Look," she said, pointing to the TV in the sitting area across the room.

I turned to see Daphne Littleton live in front of Stone Mountain.

I moved over to the TV. In another moment, Summer was beside me.

"Even with Wayne Williams behind bars," she was saying, "Atlanta is once again a city under siege."

The mountain loomed large behind her, the north-face carving dim but visible in the night.

"That's—she's set up in our parking lot," Summer said. "Has to be."

"For now the park will remain open," Daphne was saying. "But there is an additional police presence and the public, in particular young women, are being warned to use extreme caution."

"John," Daphne said as I walked up.

She had just finished her report and was still holding the mic within the bright circle of illumination from the camera lights.

"How about an on-camera interview?" she said.

I shook my head.

"It won't be live. We'll just do a quick interview to include in my next report."

"You know the answer," I said.

"Can't blame a girl for trying," she said, handing the camera guy her mic and stepping over to me.

"Your report this evening almost cost me my job," I said.

"Really? Why?"

"Because of your little stunt at lunch today. Everyone thought I was your source."

"Oh, shit, sorry. Do you want me to let your boss know it wasn't you? I won't tell him who it was, but I don't mind telling him it wasn't you."

I shook my head. "They wouldn't believe you."

"Really?"

"And it's not just that they think you lie for a living—"

"*Lie*?"

"Well . . . disseminate partial truths and dangerous misinformation. How's that?"

"Not any better, no," she said. "Damn."

"They'd think you were protecting your source," I said.

"Well, I'm sorry. I truly am. Didn't mean to jam you up."

"You can make it up to me—"

"Yes, I can."

"By telling me who your source really was."

"Sure," she said. "Since it's you. My source is . . . someone close to the investigation."

23

After leaving Daphne, I decided to check in with Joe Ross over at the campground.

On the drive over, I rolled down my windows and took in the mountain and the surrounding park.

The five-mile-around and 1,686-feet-high quartz monzonite dome is stunning to behold—even at night. It rises up out of the earth a huge solid stone. Massive. Unique. Immovable.

The most striking feature of Stone Mountain is that most of its surface is bare rock and rock pools. The lower slopes are wooded, but the enormous dome is mostly hard, solid, bare, rough rock.

Formed over three hundred million years ago by an upwelling from within the earth's crust of magma that cooled and crystalized and solidified to form granite, Stone Mountain is a pluton—a body of intrusive igneous rock named after Pluto, the god of the underworld.

The Stone Cold Killer isn't the first evil force to be drawn to this giant geological spectacle. On Thanksgiving eve in 1915 sixteen men climbed the mountain and lit a towering cross on fire. It was the rebirth of the Ku Klux Klan.

Mountains have always drawn humanity, for both noble and evil pursuits. Stone Mountain has its own energy, a powerful force that attracts the best and worst of us.

When I arrived at Joe's campsite, he wasn't there. Ember and ash were still hot in his fire pit, but there was no sign of him.

Something about his campsite seemed off, but I couldn't figure out exactly what it was.

There was an excessive amount of fishing equipment scattered about—both next to his tent and in his truck—poles, rod and reels, nets, knives, tackle boxes, and I wondered if he was here to work or fish.

His truck was here, so wherever he went he went on foot—or got a ride with someone else.

While I waited for him, I decided to look around the area.

RVs and tents were lined up around loops off of Stonewall Jackson Drive in outcroppings of land, the jagged tips of which were in Stone Mountain Lake. Nearly all the camp sites had fires or places for them. Nearly all had vehicles in front of them—and bicycles, canoes, and kayaks scattered about them, and though all the sites were rustic and picturesque beneath Georgia pines and with a view of the east side of the mountain, the sites actually on the lake were by far the best.

The entire secluded area was serene, relaxing and restorative, and it was difficult to fathom a cold-hearted killer who abducts and terrifies and tortures and murders young women in such a horrific way feeling at home here.

When I got back to Joe's campsite and found that he still hadn't returned, I decided to leave and come back later.

I could feel myself being drawn back to the inn, to Summer who would be up all night and be a welcome companion for lonely insomniac hours, and by telling myself I'd come back later to check on Joe I was rationalizing and justifying why I should stay out here tonight.

"I'm so glad you came back," Summer said. "I didn't think you were going to. You gonna take me up on my offer of a bed to crash in?"

I shrugged. "Might. But nowhere near sleepy yet."

She smiled knowingly and as it had when I had been with her before, Edward Hopper's Nighthawks popped into my head.

"There's coffee and booze in the bar," she said. "And I have a key."

"Cool," I said. "Let me make a phone call first, then I'll get us set up."

"Here," she said. "Come around here and use this phone while I run to the little girls' room. Just push this button for an outside line and if a call comes in don't worry about it. They'll call back. They always do."

While she was in the restroom in the back of the lobby, I called Susan.

"Just closing up," she said. "You home? I'm heading that way."

"Still out at the mountain," I said. "Joe's camping out here—doing surveillance of the campgrounds, but when I went to check on him, he wasn't there. I'm gonna go back and check on him again in a little while. Make sure he's okay. Depending on how late it is when I finally find him I may just crash out here."

"Really?" she asked, her voice full of sadness and disappointment.

"Yeah, you'll be sound asleep by the time I could get there."

"But I like having you sleeping next to me."

"I know and I may still come crawl in bed later, but . . ."

"Okay, well, be careful. Please be careful."

When Summer returned from the restroom, she said, "Pick your poison. Caffeine or alcohol?"

"Give me the keys and I'll surprise you."

"I was thinking . . ." she said. "Do you think the killer is . . .

How do you think he's getting the girls up the mountain? Does he force them to walk up it at gunpoint? Does he knock them out and carry them? Can you imagine the strength required to do that? I think he might be far, far more formidable than we even imagined."

24

The next morning I woke up in Summer's bed with a raging headache and a hangover—and though I was alone and had been, an overwhelming sense of guilt.

The headline of the newspaper on the hallway floor in front of the door read Stone Cold Killer Terrorizes Atlanta's Stone Mountain.

Out in the parking lot and along Robert E. Lee Boulevard TV news vans, with satellites and antennas extended, were lined up, reporters and camera crews broadcasting with the mountain in the background over their padded shoulders.

But the most surprising and disturbing development of all was waiting for me at the department.

"This was slid under the door sometime last night," Bud said, handing me a letter inside a clear plastic evidence bag.

To the Poor Cops,

This is the Stone Cold Killer.

You are way behind and don't seem to be catching up very well so I am going to give you some help. I know you think that with all the attention on the mountain I will not take another girl. It would be suicide, right? All the TV cameras and reporters watching. All the cops on patrol. All the citizen sleuths trying to catch me. The whole world is watching and yet I will do it again and you will not be able to stop me or even catch me. I know you want to kill me, but you are not up to the task. I am as immovable as Stone Mountain. You will see. You can't stop me. Only I can stop me and I am not going to stop me. Just you wait. You will see with your own eyes what I will do. Behold my work and tremble. Recognize what you are dealing with and show me the respect I am owed. If you don't I will punish you. I promise. Poor cops. You are weak and slow and inept. You are no match for me. Your rightful job now is just to bear witness to my work. That is all. Though I wonder if you can even do that.

Sincerely,
S.C.K.

"Evidently he likes the name Daphne came up with for him," I said.

"How do you know she came up with it?" Walt said.

"Because in her report she said cops were calling him that and none of us are. She made it up—like a lot of what she reported. It's what she does."

Before he could say anything else, Frank walked in looking frayed and frazzled. "Sorry I'm late," he said. "Lots of fires to put out."

I had been around Frank when he was investigating other intense, high-profile cases before, but I had never seen him like this.

"Whatta we got?" he asked.

I handed him the letter.

He read it.

"Did you see the paper this morning?" Bud asked him.

He nodded. "Any hope we had of an unimpeded investigation

is now over. Straight circus from here on out. Gonna make everything harder."

Even as we were in here having this discussion, a pool of reporters was right outside the front door, demanding a statement, hurling questions to every cop coming and going. Another, larger group of them was still inside the park.

Bud said, "We've got media everywhere—not just local. National too. We've got psychics and other law enforcement agencies offering help. And the phone hasn't stopped ringing with tips from potential witnesses, many saying they think they know who the killer is."

"I've got more GBI agents wanting to help now too," Frank said. "We're gonna need the extra help to respond to leads and manage the media. We'll just have to get organized and assign different tasks to different officers and agencies and just coordinate very carefully. Have regular meetings to update each other on what's going on, but our core group will remain intact and working together on it."

Bud nodded. "Appreciate that," he said. "It's takin' place in our backyard. We'd like to be the ones to bring this bastard down."

Frank nodded, then looked over at me. "What do you make of this?" he asked holding up the letter. To the others he said, "John's been working with an FBI-trained profiler."

"There's something about it that . . . Something about it bothers me, but I can't quite get it to finish developing. Come back to me."

As they continued to talk about it and reread it, I began to think about why it didn't sit quite right with me.

I had learned to let go of thoughts, to stop so focusing on or chasing one that others couldn't come, so I just let go. Putting my mind into neutral . . . I gazed within, my inner eyes wide and unfocused, searching for movement in the dimness.

Flashes of Summer's naked body streaked the night sky of my mind, though I had never seen her without her clothes.

Feelings of guilt and thoughts of Susan followed.

Then . . .

Unbidden, images and remembrances from some of my recent classes came to mind.

And I began to think about my changing concepts of God and religion and the Bible.

As a child I had been taught that the Bible was written by God, that its pages contained his message to humanity. The more I learned about the complex and diverse group of books—written by hundreds of people over thousands of years, the more I discovered what it actually is.

By viewing the Bible as a single, divinely-inspired book, the question quickly arises why does the God within its pages seem to so often contradict him or herself? Why does God say one thing at one time and the exact opposite at another?

The conclusion I had reached lately was that the Bible wasn't so much a message from God but the thoughts and theories, hopes and fears, of humanity projected onto God. God could sound like two different beings, contradictory and diametrically opposed to each other because two or more different people had written the passages. The rigid and paranoid and mistrusting would write an angry, vengeful God while the kind and generous and ecumenical would portray a God of love and mercy and generosity.

And I realized what bothered me about the note was that it seemed to contradict the image I had of the killer based on his actions up until now. Was it written by someone else or did I have a misconception of the killer or was the killer trying to sound other than what he was?

Frank looked over at me. "You've got something, don't you?"

I shrugged. "Maybe. The letter doesn't fit with what we were thinking about him," I said. "I wouldn't have expected him to contact us. What he's doing seems personal, almost private. He committed at least four that we know of in secrecy. I realize there are elements of what he's doing that are . . . But I wouldn't have said he was a thrill killer, wouldn't have expected him to taunt us the way he did, wouldn't have expected him to make this a contest and tell us he was going to do it again with everyone watching."

"So you were wrong about him?" Walt said. "All that profile shit sounds like a bunch of bullshit to me anyway. Always has."

"Or," Erin said, "the letter wasn't from the killer."

Frank looked at me and raised his eyebrows. "Which is it?"

I shrugged. "I'm not sure. I'd like to get Ernestine Campbell's take on it, but . . . it could be both. It could be that he's smart enough, knows enough, to pretend to be something other than what he really is in the letter. Or it could be like the Dear Boss letter or Saucy Jack postcard versus the From Hell letter."

"The what?" Erin asked.

"Letters supposedly sent from Jack the Ripper," I said. "Very different in tone and content. The Dear Boss letter and Saucy Jack postcard are most likely fakes—someone pretending to be the ripper, but the From Hell letter is believed by many to be from the actual killer."

I then told them as best I could from memory some of the key components of the three pieces of correspondence.

Dear Boss,

I keep on hearing the police have caught me but they wont fix me just yet. I have laughed when they look so clever and talk about being on the right track. That joke about Leather Apron gave me real fits. I am down on whores and I shant quit ripping them till I do get buckled. Grand work the last job was. I gave the lady no time to squeal. How can they catch me now. I love my work and want to start again. You will soon hear of me with my funny little games. I saved some of the proper red stuff in a ginger beer bottle over the last job to write with but it went thick like glue and I cant use it. Red ink is fit enough I hope ha. ha. The next job I do I shall clip the ladys ears off and send to the police officers just for jolly wouldn't you. Keep this letter back till I do a bit more work, then give it out straight. My knife's so nice and sharp I want to get to work right away if I get a chance. Good Luck. Yours truly

Jack the Ripper

Dont mind me giving the trade name

PS Wasnt good enough to post this before I got all the red ink off my hands curse it. No luck yet. They say I'm a doctor now. ha ha

I was not codding dear old Boss when I gave you the tip, you'll hear about Saucy Jacky's work tomorrow double event this time number one squealed a bit couldn't finish straight off. Had not got time to get ears off for police thanks for keeping last letter back till I got to work again.

Jack the Ripper

From hell.

Mr Lusk,

Sor

I send you half the Kidne I took from one woman prasarved it for you tother piece I fried and ate it was very nise. I may send you the bloody knif that took it out if you only wate a whil longer

signed

Catch me when you can Mishter Lusk

I then explained to them the best I could the differences in the personality types and criminal profiles of the various writers of the two letters and postcard. Dear Boss and Saucy Jack are flamboyant, taunting, and braggadocios. They are also addressed to large agencies, unlike the From Hell letter, which is addressed to an individual—George Lusk, the chairman of the Whitechapel Vigilance Committee. It also does not use the flashy Jack the Ripper moniker, which was already in the public sphere when the letter was written.

Frank pursed his lips and nodded, seeming to think about it.

No one said anything for a moment.

"There's something . . ." I started. "Does the letter remind you of anything?"

I had directed the question toward Frank, but they all responded with shrugs or shakes of their heads.

"Like he's trying to sound like someone," I said. "Something about it reminds me of the Zodiac's letters."

"You think it's the fuckin' Zodiac doin' it?" Walt said.

I frowned and shook my head. "No. Like maybe he copied the style of letter."

Bud yelled out at Miss D. "Miss D, you still got that Zodiac paperback?"

"Lent it to Connie next door, Chief. Want me to go get it from her?"

"Would you please?"

Within a matter of minutes, Miss D was handing Bud a small book—not a paperback like he had thought, but a beat up St. Martin's hardcover with a black tattered cover and dust jacket with the symbol of the Zodiac in white on it, its pages dog-eared, its spine turned at an odd angle.

Bud handed it right back to her. "Find me his letters."

She turned right to them.

"Read us one," he said.

She nodded. "'This is the Zodiac speaking. I am the murderer of the taxi driver over by Washington Street plus Maple Street last night, to prove this here is a blood stained piece of his shirt. I am the same man who did in the people in the north bay area. The S.F. Police could have caught me last night if they had searched the park properly instead of holding road races with their motorcicles seeing who could make the most noise. The car drivers should have just parked their cars and sat there quietly waiting for me to come out of cover. School children make nice targets, I think I shall wipe out a school bus some morning. Just shoot out the front tire then pick off the kiddies as they come bouncing out.'"

"I don't know . . ." Bud said. "Does that sound the same to y'all?"

Erin and Joe shrugged.

Walt shook his head. "Don't to me."

Frank nodded. "I can hear it. There's something to the flatness and cadence of it. I can see why it made you think of it."

"Thank you, Miss D," Bud said.

She sat the book down on his desk and walked out.

A moment later she walked right back in. "Chief, think you need to see this."

25

We all followed Miss D out of Bud's office and into the squad room and gathered around the old television.

A shot of Daphne Littleton standing in front of Stone Mountain filled the screen.

"Again, this is a WSB-TV exclusive," she was saying. "This reporter has managed to get a copy of a letter the Stone Cold Killer sent the police this morning. It says, and I quote, 'To the Poor Cops. This is the Stone Cold Killer. You are way behind and don't seem to be catching up very well so I am going to give you some help—'"

"What the hell?" Bud said. "How in the hell did she get her hands on . . ."

Everyone but Frank and Bud looked at me.

I shook my head. "No way. Wasn't me. I didn't even know anything about it until I came in a little while ago and y'all showed it to me."

"It wasn't John," Frank said.

"Who then?" Bud said. "Someone with access to our department, damn it. Who would—"

"Maybe," I said. "But it's at least as likely that the killer sent it to her."

"Son of a bitch," Walt said.

Frank nodded. "I bet you're right."

"'I am as immovable as Stone Mountain,'" Daphne was reading. "'You will see. You can't stop me. Only I can stop me and I am not going to stop me. Just you wait. You will see with your own eyes what I will do. Behold my work and tremble.'"

"We've lost all control now," Frank said. "All control."

Over the next few days, as Susan and I grew more and more estranged, the investigation continued without much in the way of breakthroughs.

We attended funerals and visitations, observed and took pictures of those in attendance.

We searched through the credit card receipts of Stone Mountain Park.

We fielded countless calls from coworkers and family members and landlords saying they knew who the killer was.

We followed lead after lead into dead end after dead end.

We took calls and read letters from psychics.

Joe Ross continued to camp in the park, continued not to be at his tent when I stopped by to check on him, and I wondered if he were doing more fishing, hiking, and camping than working. This part of the investigation may well amount to little more than a paid vacation for him.

We all continued to patrol and observe and stakeout.

And I continued to find reasons to sleep in Summer's bed.

One afternoon while Erin and I were going through more credit card receipts from the park at a table in the department conference room, Susan showed up unexpectedly.

"Is everything okay?" I asked. "Did something happen?"

"Can I talk to you a minute?"

I stood. "Yeah, sure, let's go in—"

"Stay in here," Erin said. "I need a break anyway. You want a soda or coffee or anything?"

"I'm okay," I said. "Thanks. Susan?"

She shook her head.

After Erin left the room and closed the door behind her I said, "What's going on?"

"I never see you anymore," she said. "Figured this was the best way."

"Best way for what?"

"To see you. To talk to you."

"You just want to talk? Why don't I come by Scarlett's tonight or we go to dinner or something?"

"Because you won't and we can't really talk there anyway. I won't take too much of your precious investigation time, but I want to talk to you now."

"Okay. Do you want to sit?"

She shook her head.

I waited but she didn't say anything.

She looked, as she did most of the time these days, tired and a little frazzled. Standing there looking at her I realized again that I just wasn't attracted to her—at least not in the way I wanted to be. I wasn't saying she wasn't attractive, just that I wasn't drawn to her, that I felt no particular pull—not physically or sexually, not emotionally or mentally. And I had felt this . . . this lack of desire long before I had encountered Summer Grantham again and began to feel it for her.

"Are you . . ." I began. "Do you . . . want to . . . what's on your mind?"

"Don't rush me."

"I'm not."

She took a deep breath and let it out in a big sigh. "I feel like . . . Are you trying to get me to break up with you?"

"What? Why would you ask that?"

"Just answer the—I feel like you're trying to find an off-ramp but . . . you don't want to be the one to . . . so you want me to end it."

I wasn't consciously trying to get her to end our relationship, but hearing her say it I wondered if subconsciously that wasn't exactly what I wanted.

"Are you happy?" I asked. "I mean with . . . our . . . with us?"

"Not lately, no," she said. "I never see you anymore. It's like we don't have a relationship. But answer my question."

I shook my head. "No, I haven't been trying to get you to break up with me, but I'm not happy either. And I know we haven't seen each other as much since I started working this case, but we didn't see each other a whole lot before. We went from very little time together to none at all."

"Can't you change that?" she asked.

I shrugged. "Somewhat, I guess, but for what? I'd work on this case less to going back to getting a few minutes with you each night while you're fighting to stay awake?"

"Yeah. Give us at least that."

"The truth is . . . long before I started working this case . . . you made a decision to help your aunt every night instead of giving us a . . . chance at a . . ."

"What, I'm not supposed to help her?"

"Not all night every night," I said. "You're enabling her. I recognize it because you do it for me."

"So I should just let her business fail?"

"No," I said, "you should let us."

"You're blaming me for . . . us failing?"

I shook my head. "No. I'm not. I don't mean to."

"I should've never gotten you this job."

"What? *You* got me this job?"

"Yeah. What? You think you got it on your own, Mr. Super Detective? You were drinking so much, you were bored and restless so I called Frank."

I couldn't speak.

"Of course I got you this job. I'm an enabler, remember? Consider it a parting gift, a consolation prize. And the next time you're feeling like you're Sherlock Holmes, ask yourself why that never even crossed your mind . . . or why you have no idea what's going on with Frank."

26

They were so fascinating, these gullible and unsuspecting humans.

So trusting. So careless. So clueless.

Death was brushing up against them and they didn't have the slightest inkling.

Mask of sanity was still in place.

Human suit was still on and extremely effective.

It seemed as though everyone in the world was looking for him right now, but because of his years of discipline and training, of careful study of what the expression of human emotion and normal behavior looked like, he was passing for human, passing by right between them.

If they only knew . . . he'd win an award.

He had the perfect role and was playing the part to perfection.

All the world's a stage.

Never a truer statement where he was concerned. Always hidden. Always on. Always in the role of a lifetime. Until he wasn't and when he wasn't it meant the rare individual who witnessed it was not long for this world.

When I lift my mask and she gets to really see me . . . she's not going to see much of anything else after that.

Behold. What a thing of awe and wonder he was. What a thing to behold. Fitting for the final thing they would see.

He'd been patiently bringing along the next young woman who would behold his true essence. She was almost ready, almost ripe. For now though she was still serving his purposes, but soon her usefulness would end and so too would her existence.

He couldn't wait for the moment of unveiling. Couldn't wait to see the look on her face, the surprise in her wide eyes, the gasping gape of her stunned mouth. And through her the whole world would see, would behold.

She was serving her purpose in life. She would soon serve her purpose in death.

And she had no idea.

The irony was . . . she thought she was using him. She was cunning and manipulative, but she was no match for him. And she didn't even know it. She thought she was a predator, but she was just prey, just like all the rest.

How much more self-deceived could you get—prey prancing around feeling like a predator.

27

It took a while—probably because, as Susan said, I wasn't the detective I thought I was—but I finally managed to track Frank down at Grady Hospital.

He was in a small surgical waiting room sitting by himself, his head tilted back at an awkward, uncomfortable angle, bobbing slightly as he'd doze off and jerk awake.

I sat down beside him.

There were only two other people in the room and they were about as far away from us as they could be and still be in the room.

"How'd you find me?" he asked. "Did something happen? A break in the case?"

I shook my head. "Just came to sit with you."

"Oh."

"Why didn't you tell me?" I asked.

His wife, Sylvia, had been ill for over a month now and so far they hadn't found a doctor who could tell them why.

"You got enough going on," he said. "'Sides . . . nothin' to tell so far. They can't tell us a *goddamn* thing."

It was the first time I had heard him use language like that.

"I'm so sorry," I said.

"Test after test after test . . ." he said. "Putting her poor body through so much and for . . . nothing. Nothing. No closer to knowin' now than we were when we first went to the first damn doctor. Sorry . . . I just . . ."

"Don't be," I said. "Only thing you should be sorry for is not telling me. Not letting me help with . . . something."

He frowned and seemed to think but didn't say anything.

"And it's not just helping . . ." I said. "Even if there's nothing I can do . . . you should've told me because . . . because . . . you're . . . the closest thing to a dad I've got right now."

He sniffled and blinked several times.

"Anyway," I said. "I know now . . . and I'm here. I'm not going anywhere."

"I'm . . . I appreciate that," he said. "More than you'll ever know. But . . . I need you working the case. That's how you can help me the most right now. I can't do what I want to on it. I need you working it and keeping me up to speed with what's going on with it."

I shook my head. "I . . . You don't have to say that," I said. "Susan told me you just got me involved because she asked you to."

"What?"

I nodded.

"She said what?" he said.

I told him what she had told me.

"That's not . . . She called me and said you had been drinking a good bit and she was worried about you, could I check on you. That was it. She didn't ask me to find you a job or get your help on a case. I had already decided to ask for your help before she called and would have anyway if she hadn't. In fact, I would have sooner—even before she called—if I hadn't been dealing with this."

He gestured toward the hospital.

"I don't know why she would tell you something like that," he said. "Maybe she really believes it, but . . . it's not true. The truth is I need your help now more than ever. We've got to catch this bastard before he kills another young girl. I have to be here. I can't . . . not be here waiting . . . even just waiting, so . . . go do that . . . thing you do. Put that mind of yours to work on this and help me find him before he kills again."

28

That afternoon we got our first real break in the case.

It was the result of careful, tedious, investigative police work.

I was in Bud's office talking to him about Frank when Erin walked in holding a file folder.

Bud's office wasn't as 1960s looking as he was in his black slacks, white button-down, crewcut, and black horn-rimmed glasses, but it certainly didn't appear to have ever been updated since it was built in the '70s.

"Got it," she said.

When Walt saw her, he motioned to Joe and they joined us.

"What's that?" Bud asked.

"We've been through all the receipts from the park," she said. "Only three men were in the park around the time all four women were murdered."

"Unless he paid cash," Walt said.

"Yes," she said. "And he probably did, but . . . who knows . . . killers make mistakes."

"If they didn't," Bud said, "we'd never catch them."

"Maybe he thought he had cash, but didn't," she said. "Maybe he ran out and still needed to hydrate or eat something because it took longer than he thought it was going to or . . . I don't know."

"It's good work," Bud said. "We've got to check them out, interview them. Find out everything we can about them. What are the chances that one of them's not the killer? Think about it. We've got three guys in the park all four times one of the young women was killed. What are the odds?"

"Not very high," Erin said. "And it gets better."

"Oh yeah?" Bud said. "How's that?"

"One of the guys is Benton Weston," she said. "Shelly Hepola's boyfriend."

"*One of the guys who was there for all four murders is actually the boyfriend of one of the victims?*" Bud asked, his voice rising in equal parts excitement and incredulity.

"Uh huh."

"No," he said. "That's not a coincidence. That's a . . . I don't know what that is, but that's not a coincidence."

"Got to be him," Walt said.

"Treat all of them like it's them," Bud said. "Do everything by the book. Don't cut any corners. Don't let any of them rattle you. Treat each one with respect and dignity. Don't do anything that could get evidence thrown out or a claim of police misconduct. And don't just focus on the boyfriend. We've got two other guys who were also there. Act as if each one was the only one. Understand?"

We all nod.

"Yes, sir," Erin said.

"I'll get with Frank and we'll come up with an interview strategy and decide who's going to conduct the interviews and we'll put a plan in place. Then—"

"I want to be in the room," Walt said.

"We all do," Joe said.

"Joe's right," Bud said. "We all do, but we've got to go with whoever gives us the best chance of getting him. I suspect it won't be any of us. I'm sure the GBI has specially trained interviewers who know exactly how to get a confession or at least enough contradictions . . . so we can—so at trial the prosecutor can demonstrate he's lying, impeach him with his own testimony."

"It should be one of us," Walt said.

"No," Bud said, "it should be whoever gives us our best chance at getting him."

"But—"

"Son, let me tell you something," Bud said. "Innocent young women with their whole lives ahead of them went for a run—a run—that's it. These were good girls, not doing anything or anybody wrong. They just went for a run. And a monster jumped out of the dark and tortured and murdered them—in our town, in a place we're supposed to pro—the young women were people we were supposed to protect. So I can't . . . I'm not gonna let pride or ego or turf guarding or anything—"

"You just said it was our town, our responsibility," Walt said.

"It's my responsibility to secure a conviction, to stop this . . . this . . . and I'm gonna do whatever I have to to do just that. End of discussion."

"There's something else," Erin said.

"What's that?" Bud said.

"Someone else we know was in the park during all four . . . abductions and . . . Well, actually several someones. I got to thinking. These three aren't the only ones who were in the park during all four . . . murders. So were the workers—the people who work in the park. So I looked at them too."

"Damn, girl," Walt said. "What are you? Some kind of cop or something."

"Good work," Bud said. "Good thinking."

I thought about Bobby Meredith and the other Stone Mountain Park Police. They were also always around, in the park, when the abductions and murders had taken place. I was reminded of how many killers like the one we were after had tried and failed to be cops, how many had become security guards or police buffs—hanging out at the station or the local bar frequented by cops, or inserting themselves into the case in some way. I remembered how much Ed Kemper, the Co-ed Killer, had wanted to be a state trooper and how he had spent so much time at the Santa Cruz cop bar he was thought of as a friendly nuisance. I had all these thoughts and had every intention of doing something about them, to look into Bobby Meredith and the others, but I'd get busy with other aspects of the investigation and fail to follow up and that would be a fatal flaw in my handling of this case, one that would cost me far more than I could fathom.

"We need to look more closely at all of them," she said, "but one of the guys has been tried for assault and rape before. He got off, so he doesn't have a record, but . . . it was a technicality. I think he did it. And what if he's still doing it? What if he has escalated?"

29

"I've been waiting for y'all to show up," Patrick Dorsey said.

He was a tall, thin man with a sun-damaged face and a long gray ponytail. His fine gray hair had receded to about the halfway point of his smallish head which made his long ponytail look all the more out of place.

Patrick Dorsey worked for Stone Mountain Park maintenance and in the past had been accused of assault and rape.

Walt and I were interviewing him while Erin, Joe, Frank, Bud, and two GBI agents were reaching out to the other suspects.

Frank had been advised by his interview expert on how to proceed and that was how we were doing it—each man would be interviewed in the field by two members of the task force. If it warranted follow-up, formal interviews would be conducted at the station by a GBI agent who specialized in them.

I didn't want to be partnered with Walt, but I wasn't given a choice.

"Knew the minute I seen the report on the TV news," Dorsey was saying, "it was just a matter of time 'til somebody knocked on my door."

We hadn't exactly knocked on his door. We had driven up to

his worksite on the east side of the mountain and asked to speak to him.

I wasn't sure what they were working on, but several men in yellow hardhats were scattered about—as was heavy equipment, white and green PVC pipe, and large wooden crates.

"Then you know why we're here," Walt said.

Dorsey nodded.

He was still wearing his thick leather work gloves, hardhat, and dark knockoff aviator shades.

"Mind removing your sunglasses?" Walt said.

Dorsey took off his gloves and shoved them in his jacket pocket, then removed his shades, folded the arms, hooking one of them over the neck of his sweatshirt.

"Do you have an alibi for the time of the murders?" I asked.

He nodded. "I certainly do."

"How do you even know when they were?" Walt said.

"Well, whenever they were I got an alibi and I'a tell you why. 'Cause I didn't do it. Simple as that. Never killed anybody in my life."

"Tell me about the assault and rape charges," Walt said a little too loudly.

We had walked some fifteen feet away from where the men were working, but not so far that they couldn't hear that.

"Come on, man," Dorsey said. "No need for that shit. I'm cooperating. Answering your questions. Haven't asked for a lawyer."

"You're not under arrest," Walt said. "Not entitled to a lawyer."

"Everybody's entitled to an attorney, man. It's the American way."

"We'll talk more quietly," I said. "Just answer our questions honestly. We're not looking to jam you up."

"I don't know . . ." Walt said. "I hate a fuckin' rapist."

"I ain't a rapist, man. That was a misunderstanding. That's all. We were high as fuckin' kites, man. Neither of us knew what we were doing. It was my old lady's best friend and after she realized what we'd done in a more sober state of mind she freaked. Rather than admit to her friend that she fucked her husband, she . . . claimed I raped her. Swear to God. That was it. She destroyed my life but she saved her friendship. Women, man, right?"

"And the assault?" he said.

"Both of 'em jumped me. I didn't assault anyone. I defended myself from some serious fucking bodily harm. One of the investigating officers called it what it was. Scorned women bullshit. He'll tell you. Give him a call."

"We will. What's his name and number?"

He produced a small card with both on it a little too quickly.

"That was awful fast and convenient," Walt said. "Got that shit on speed dial, don't he?"

"Like I said . . . been expecting you."

"We'll check it out," Walt said. "Meantime don't go anywhere and don't even look at any women around here. Understand?"

"All too well, man. All too well."

30

When we reached our vehicle, Daphne Littleton and her camera man were pulling up in their news van.

The camera man was named Stan and everyone referred to him as Stan the Camera Man. He was overweight and slovenly, had long, bush black hair and needed a shave.

Walt looked at me. "Your little friend with the big tits is here."

"She's not my friend," I said. "And she's not here for me."

Stan the Camera Man, who also served as Daphne's driver and security guard—something often needed for the pushy and unpopular reporter—parked behind us, blocking us in on the narrow access road.

"What're y'all doing back here?" Daphne asked as she jumped out of the van. "Is it another body?"

"What the fuck is wrong with you?" I said.

"*What*?" she asked, recoiling at my language and tone.

She had never heard me say anything like that before. Few people had. I rarely if ever spoke that way.

As we were talking, Stan had climbed out of the driver's door, rushed around the back of the van, opened the panel on the side, and was readying his camera equipment. When he heard the way

I spoke to Daphne, he stopped what he was doing and turned toward us.

"How can you sound excited about the prospects of another innocent young woman being tortured and murdered?"

"I didn't think they were tortured," she said. "Are they . . . Does he torture them?"

She was obviously asking out of excitement for a new story angle, not concern.

"I'm talking about mental, emotional, psychological torture," I said. "The unimaginable terror that comes from being abducted, feeling powerless, being held against your will. I'm talking about the horror of knowing you're going to die."

"Oooh, that's good. I can use that."

"No you can't," I said. "But I do have a quote for you."

"Great. Hold on a minute and let me get my camera. Stan, get over here."

Stan arrived a moment later, camera on his shoulder, mic held out to her.

She took the mic and thrusted it out toward me.

"We're rolling," Stan said.

She turned toward the camera and said, "This is a WSB-TV exclusive. I'm Daphne Littleton. I'm here with two of the police officers working the Stone Cold Killer case. Detective Jordan what can you tell us about the case?"

"That a reporter who derives pleasure from the death of young women is not dissimilar to the psychopath killing them. The two aberrations of humanity are on the same antisocial spectrum."

"Stop the camera," Walt said.

Stan didn't respond.

"Hey. Fatboy. I said stop the camera and move your fuckin' van. Now."

Ignoring him, Daphne asked me, "If you're not back here because of a body . . . Are you interviewing someone? A witness or a suspect? Is it a suspect? Who is it? Does the killer work at the park? Is he in maintenance? What's his name? The people have a right to hear what he has to say."

"From a behavioral standpoint," I said. "The only suspect that fits the profile so far is Daphne Littleton. You should definitely talk to her. The people have a right to hear what she has to say."

"You think this is a joke?" she said.

Walt said, "We think you are. Now move your goddamn van now or I'm gonna arrest you and give an exclusive to Channel Five."

"I'm serious, John. Y'all need me on your side. Do you have any idea how bad I can make you look if I want to? Or how bad it'd look if I solved this thing instead of y'all?"

Walt drew his weapon and grabbed his cuffs off his belt. "Okay," he said. "Very slowly, put the mic and the camera down and lace your hands behind your head."

Stepping out from behind the van, seeming to materialize out of thin air, Bobby Meredith said, "I got this, Walt. Little time in our cell works wonders for uppity bitches."

"We're going. We're going," Daphne said. "Jesus. Y'all're gonna threaten to arrest a member of the media for doing her job."

"It's not a threat," Meredith said. "It's happening. Now put the—"

She turned and started walking away. "Come on Stan. We're through here."

Stan glanced at Walt, who had his gun out but wasn't pointing it at them, then back to Bobby Meredith, then followed Daphne.

They returned their equipment to the back of the van, got in, and began to back down the service road. And Walt and Bobby let them.

31

When we got back to the station, Frank and Bud were already back.

"Well?" Frank said.

"Claims to be innocent," Walt said. "Said he was havin' an affair with his wife's best friend and rather than admit it, the best friend cried rape."

"Y'all buyin' it?" Bud asked.

I shook my head. "Not without some major substantial corroborating evidence. I mean, it's possible he's telling some version of the truth, but . . . I don't know."

"He's lying his ass off," Walt said.

"He wasn't convicted for some reason," I said. "We need to find out what it was. Be good to talk to the victim too."

"Yeah," Walt said. "What he said."

"But," I said, "even if he's lying, even if he's guilty of rape and assault . . . that's a long way from what the killer in this case is doing. Doesn't even appear to be about rape."

"True," Frank said.

I saw a flash of something just then, an image that might be part of the solution to catching him, but . . . it was gone just as fast as it had come and I couldn't get it back. What had made me think of it, what had I said or heard or thought that . . . It was when I said these murders don't appear to have anything to do with rape.

Why? What is significant about that?

I'd have to file it away for when I could really give it a good think.

"Sounds like it's worth following up," Frank said, "but not our highest priority. Agree?"

I nodded. "Should be able to get what we need with a couple of phone calls. Investigator or DA and the victim. I'll try to track them down this evening."

"Thanks."

I wanted to ask him how Sylvia's tests went but didn't want to do it front of the others. I'd have to remember to check with him before he left or call him tonight if we didn't get a moment alone before then.

"Y'all get anywhere with y'all's?" Walt asked.

Frank shook his head. "Mine works out of town a few days a week. I left a message for him. We'll see if he calls back. If not, we'll pay him a return visit this weekend."

Frank had Randy North, one of the three men who had visited the park on the same days the four victims had been murdered.

"My guy's in a wheelchair," Bud said. "Goes to Stone Mountain to walk his dog. Got one of those motorized chairs. Says he's out there most every day."

Bud had Teddy Sears.

"Could he be faking?" I asked. "Using the wheelchair as a cover?"

"That's what I wondered," he said. "Seemed real to me, but I've got a call into his doctor. So we'll see."

Something occurred to me then.

"I know we've got Joe staying at the campground and keeping

an eye on things," I said, "but has anyone checked to see if anyone has been camping either this entire time or at least each time the young women were taken?"

"We need to do that," Bud said.

"Good thinking, John," Frank said. "Whether they pay in cash or with a credit card, they have to register, so we should be able to tell pretty quickly and easily. I'll get somebody over there tonight."

"I checked the registration records at the inn," I said. "None of the guests have stayed the entire time or been here every time one of the women went missing."

Walt started to say something but stopped when Joe and Erin walked in.

"Y'all aren't going to believe this," Erin said.

"Try us," Bud said.

"Guess who's out of the country?"

She and Joe had gone to interview Benton Weston—Shelly's boyfriend and one of the men who were in the park when she and the others were killed.

"That little fucker," Bud said. "When's he back?"

"That's the thing . . ." she said. "They say he's just on vacation, but he's got no scheduled return date."

"Son of a bitch," Walt said.

"It gets better," Joe said.

When he shook his head it emphasized his perpetual need for a haircut.

"*And* he went on a one-way ticket," she said.

"We had him and let him go," Frank said.

"Son of a bitch," Walt said.

"Oh, it gets even better," Joe said.

"He went to Vanuatu."

"Vanwhat?"

"Vanuatu," she said. "It's an island nation in the South Pacific."

"What the—" Walt started.

"Oh, it gets even better," Joe said.

"Among other things to recommend it to someone like Benton," she said, "is that it doesn't have an extradition treaty with the US."

32

That night we did another sting operation with Erin jogging around and Walt, Joe, and I following her.

Though there were far fewer walkers and runners out and about than before, there were more people. Reporters continued to roam about, their TV trucks and vans humming in the background, their headlamps and camera lights illuminating the cold, windy night.

Like the committed cop she was, Erin ran off and on for a few hours, though it was cold and she had worked all day at a stressful job.

As it approached ten, I radioed the others. "Let's call it for tonight. Erin's done enough. I don't think the killer's out here."

"Maybe if we leave," Walt said, "he'll kill a reporter."

"He ain't shown no signs he's willing to use his powers for good," Joe said. "That's just wishful thinking."

"You okay, Erin?" I asked.

"Yeah, just cold. And tired. Tired and cold. Glad we're calling it."

"Jog over to the inn," I said. "I'll follow you there and get you some hot chocolate while you change. Walt and Joe, since I'm going to the inn anyway y'all can go ahead and go if you want to."

I followed Erin over to the inn and parked, waiting a few minutes to walk in after she did.

"I'm so glad you ended it when you did," she said. "Don't know how much more I could have taken."

"You should've said something."

She shook her head. "I can't. I'm a girl. I can't ever be the first to stop anything."

"Shit, I should've thought of that," I said. "Sorry. I should've ended it sooner. We need to come up with a secret code so you can tell me what you need."

"Thank you, John. That's . . . that would be great."

"I'm disappointed in myself I didn't think of it before."

She shook her head. "None of that."

"You have time for a drink?" I asked. "I could call Summer and get her to meet us in the bar."

Summer was off tonight and waiting for me in her room.

"I'd really love that, but right now all I want to do is fall into bed."

"You want to stay here so you don't have to drive or do you want me to drive you? Summer can follow in my car and drive me back."

"That's so sweet, but I only live a few short miles away. I'll be fine."

"Would you call me and let me know when you get there?"

She nodded. "Sure. Thank you."

Though I had a key, I knocked on Summer's door and waited.

She opened it looking sleepily sexy in a classic rock T and jogging shorts.

"Hurry inside, it's cold," she said.

I did.

"Why'd you . . . Why didn't you use your key?"

"Knew you were in here. Didn't want to barge in on you."

"I gave it to you because I wanted you to be able to come and go as you like."

"Thanks. I know. And I appreciate it. But when you're here . . . I just . . . it's your room. Just being respectful."

This was the first night she had been off since I started staying here and it was odd and awkward for us to both be in the room at the same time.

"Would you rather me stay somewhere else tonight?" I asked.

"Why're you being so . . . of course not."

"Just making sure. You've been so generous with your room, but I don't want to intrude or—"

"You're being silly. I want you here. I've made it obvious."

I tried not to read too much into what she was saying, but couldn't help but wonder exactly what she meant.

You think too much, I told myself. *You worry about the wrong things. Give it a rest. At least for tonight.*

"Okay. Thank you. Mind if I jump in the shower? I'd like to warm up and freshen up."

"Help yourself. Act like it's yours, please."

33

He worked like a man possessed. He had to.

Everything had to be ready, had to be right.

Now everyone was watching . . . and boy did he have something for them to see.

This one was for them. Well, mostly for them. Okay, maybe just partially for them. He was going to enjoy it—maybe not as much as the others, as the ones that were just his, but plenty.

He loved his work. Even the preparation. Getting everything just right—the wood, the rope, the water, the ice, the tape, the gun, the knife—and of course he always had to have his mask on, his human suit.

It was going to be a long night, but well worth it. Just wait. Wait 'til the people beheld the unveiling of his work.

Wait until she did.

He couldn't wait to see the look on her face, that unmistakable moment of recognition, and then all that followed—the begging, the pleading, the bargaining, the resignation, the terror. Made him hard just imagining it.

And this time he was going to show them all just how hard he could get. He'd read a report in the paper that theorized that he was impotent since there had been no sign of rape. He'd show them just how potent he really was.

Though this one was for the little people down below, the inept cops, the reporters, and the frightened masses, he was going to savor every second of it, get as much out of it as he could. Drink it in like fine wine poured out as a drink offering.

She was waiting for him when he arrived. A big wave. A wide smile. Happy to see him.

He had to go out and get the others. This one willingly came to him.

When he got out and walked over, she actually hugged him.

Wow. The human suit holds.

He should have put this one on long ago.

Think about all you could've gotten up to over the years.

"I can't tell you how much I appreciate you doing this," she was saying. "I know some people don't understand, but . . . I'm just doing my job. But you get it, don't you? We have to stick together."

"Oh, you and I are gonna be linked together forever."

"Huh? I don't—What're you. Wait. No. No. Not you. Not you. It can't be."

34

A short while later when I walked back into the room after my shower, Summer was standing there near the end of the first bed naked.

I stopped and gazed at her, taking every inch of her in. "You're so beautiful."

"Come here," she said, holding her arms out to me.

I quickly closed the distance between us and took her in my arms.

We embraced for a long moment.

Then began kissing.

Eventually I worked my way down her neck, across her collarbone, along her shoulders and upper arms, and to her exquisite, pear-shaped breasts.

As I did, she began unbuttoning my shirt and unzipping my jeans.

I was so turned on I was finding it difficult to breathe.

When she shifted to take my shirt off, she took her breasts away from me, and I immediately experienced separation anxiety.

Grabbing my open jeans and underwear, she shimmied them

out over my erection and down to about my knees. When she stood back up she placed both her small hands on my chest and shoved me backwards and I fell onto the bed.

Once I was on the bed, she pulled my jeans and briefs the rest of the way off and took me in her mouth.

It felt as good as any sensation my young self had ever experienced, but it wasn't long before my mind kicked on and I began to be inundated with thoughts and the feelings that followed them.

At over twenty years my senior, Summer had no doubt been with many men in her forty-something rotations around the sun. Not just young men like me, but fully grown, fully filled-out men. I suddenly became self-conscious about my body. I was too skinny, too pale, too—and how did I compare size-wise to all the others?

Could I please her? Did I know enough? Would I be good enough? Could I last long enough?

Stop it. Turn off your mind and just enjoy this. Let go. Relax. Don't think about anything, just feel how good it feels.

I tried to. I really did.

But the insecure questioning that led to self-consciousness was nothing compared to pangs of guilt I began to experience.

I pictured Susan alone in the bed we had shared up until a week ago.

We weren't a good fit and it wasn't working between us, but I couldn't help but question whether I had subconsciously or not accelerated our breakup in hopes something like this would happen.

I reached down and took Summer's head in my hands, lifting and tilting it up toward me.

"I can't," I said. "I'm sorry, but . . . I just can't."

"Why?"

"I just can't."

"Your body says otherwise."

"I just got out of a relationship. It's too soon. I'm too . . ."

"Hey, it's okay. I understand," she said.

Scooting up next to me, she laid her head on my shoulder and put her arms around me.

"You're a sweet young man, John Jordan."

I didn't feel sweet. I felt frustrated, embarrassed, and pathetic. I felt guilty for being here and guilty for stopping.

I had let Susan and Summer down.

I was trying to be a man and failing miserably.

"It is too soon," she said. "And I'm sorry. I should've thought better . . . a young man as sensitive and kind as you . . . and a thinker like you are . . . of course it's too soon. Do you want us to get dressed or can we lay here like this for a few minutes?"

"Is that a trick question?" I said. "Don't dare cover up your beautiful body."

"Mine's starting to show my age," she said. "You're the one with the amazing young body."

"That's sweet."

"I'm not being sweet. Let me tell you something . . . I believe you . . . what you said about it being too soon, but if you're just saying that not to hurt my feelings . . . if I'm just too old and . . . for you . . . I understand."

I couldn't believe what I was hearing. Her forty-something-year-old self had insecurities just like my twenty-year-old self.

"Listen to me," I said. "I swear to you that that's not it. This has nothing to do with you and everything to do with me. You're so beautiful. And your body . . . You're stunning. You saw how turned on I got—how turned on I still am. This is about my own guilt and insecurity and nothing else. I'm just sorry I let you down."

"You didn't—you haven't let me down. Not in any way. All you ever do is restore my faith in the male of our species."

We talked for a short while longer, mostly continuing to reassure each other, then fell fast asleep.

In my dreams Jordan was still alive. She and I had adopted Martin Fisher and were living in a small apartment in Decatur.

I was impossibly happy.

In quick, uneven, jump-cut succession we were cooking dinner together, dancing in the kitchen, reading Martin a story before bed, making love in our own bed after a Sunday afternoon nap.

I woke with tears of happiness streaming down my cheeks and woke Summer up by making love to her.

Our groggy, passionate union was both sweet and intense and free of guilt, insecurity, and self-consciousness—all things that would no doubt creep back in later. But for now it was an exquisite, divine union.

Later, as we fell back asleep in each other's arms, I whispered, *I'm sorry* to Susan.

Both in spite of everything and because of it, I slept peacefully and soundly—until the loud banging began on the door early the next morning.

35

I jerked awake.

Waking Summer in the process.

Banging on the door.

I reached over and grabbed my gun off the nightstand.

"What is it?" Summer whispered.

"I don't know. Wait here."

I jumped out of bed and into my jeans and shirt, not bothering to button the shirt.

Rushing over to the door, I unholstered my weapon.

"John, it's Erin. Wake up."

I looked through the peephole and saw Erin Newman standing there alone.

I unchained, unlocked, and opened the door.

"What is it?" I said. "What's wrong?"

"We've got another one," she said. "She's still alive."

"Where?"

"Up on the mountain. Dangling there like she could fall at any minute."

"Let me get dressed real quick. Come in."

She stepped inside and I started getting dressed.

"Frank told me to call you at home," she said. "Didn't know if you wanted him to know about . . ." she glanced in and nodded toward the dim hotel room behind me. "I told him we worked late last night and you decided to stay here. Bud said there wasn't money in the budget for that. I told him you had a friend comp the room."

"Thanks, Erin. I really appreciate that."

Summer peeked out from the corner. "Morning."

"Morning."

After quickly getting dressed, I rushed into the bathroom and washed my face and brushed my teeth, then drank some water from the tap.

"Okay," I said, "let's go."

"Be careful," Summer said.

She had wrapped the bedspread around her and stepped into the little alcove to give me a kiss goodbye.

"And hurry back to me."

Erin and I ran down the steps and across the courtyard and around to the front of the inn, our breaths visible in the cold morning air.

Day was breaking over to our left, casting a mountain-shaped shadow to our front and right.

Everything was damp and dew-covered. And frigid.

Frank and Bud were standing there with walkie-talkies and binoculars.

Both men were on their radios.

As we approached, Frank handed me his binoculars without missing a beat in his conversation.

Erin pointed up to a place to the left side of the north face and I followed her finger with the binoculars.

There on the sheer cliff of the north side, Daphne Littleton was hanging from a large, three-strand, twisted manila rope.

Her hands were held above her head, bound at the wrists, a piece of the same rope wrapped around her ankles.

She was naked and her shivering body was lying against the cold, wet granite rock face.

The rope that wrapped around her wrists and held her in place ran up to the top of the mountain, disappearing behind a pile of boulders and a small stand of trees—one of the few spots on the giant rock where there were any.

It was difficult to tell from this perspective, but I'd guessed that the small plot of trees, bushes and rocks—the only one visible on the top of the mountain—was a half a mile or so from the famous Confederate carving.

"Is he behind the rocks?" I asked. "In the trees?"

"Yeah," Erin said. "I saw part of his arm before I went in there to get you."

"Then we've got him," I said.

"Yes we do."

Though shivering in the cold wind, it was obvious Daphne was trying not to move. She was saying something but I couldn't make it out. And her face was a mask of pure terror. Eyes wide and wild, tears streaming down her frozen face to her quivering chin.

"Okay," Frank said when he finished talking on the radio. "We've got a sky lift operator on his way in to take us up. The four of us will go up in it. Walt and Joe and several other GBI agents and Bobby Meredith and other park police are going to spread out around the perimeter and or start up the mountain. Got more cops on the way. And APD is scrambling a helicopter over here as quick as they can. This early . . . shouldn't be anyone but him on the mountain. We're blocking the entrances and exits. No one out. Only law enforcement in. Just us and him now. Let's go get the bastard."

"Has he communicated in any way?" I said. "Asked for anything?"

He shook his head. "We're concerned he'll drop her as we approach, but . . . don't feel like we can just stand down here watching, doing nothing."

I nodded. "He's gonna drop her either way," I said.

Erin nodded. "She's already dead. Best we can hope for is catching him."

"God, I hope not," Bud said, stepping over to us. "Surely we can do both."

"We're gonna try," Frank said. "We're just being realistic about the odds of a killer like this really even giving us the chance to save her."

"Then why do it like this?" Bud said.

"Why wait and give us the chance to—"

"He wants an audience," I said.

"He's risking getting caught to have one," Erin added.

"Then let's make it worth his while and catch his ass," Bud said.

36

We ran across the street and parking lot to Skyride Plaza.

One of the most popular attractions at the park is the high speed Swiss cable cars that shuttle groups of visitors to the mountain's summit and back down again. The view from the top of the mountain, which includes the city of Atlanta skyline and the Appalachian Mountains in the distance, is breathtaking, but the sights provided by the floating-on-air ride up are just as stunning.

While waiting for the operator to arrive, we stepped on the back of the platform beneath the huge damp metal structure and steel cables and attempted to get a visual on Daphne again, but the tall pine trees to our left obscured most of the mountain and blocked our view of the area where Daphne was hanging from.

"Fuck," Frank said.

We walked back over to the car.

"Come on," Frank said. "Where is he?"

"Feel so helpless just standing here," Erin said.

"Should Erin and I drive around to the west side and run up?" I asked.

"Even if it takes the operator another ten minutes to get here," Frank said, "this'll still be faster."

Bud said, "Walt and Joe are already over there. Walking up now."

Eventually, the operator sped up in his car, left it parked out in front on the curb, and ran over to us.

He was a tall, soft, pale young man in his twenties with too-long blond hair sticking up on his head.

He immediately began working on preparing the cable car to take us the over eight hundred feet to the top, which seemed to take a lot longer than it actually did.

"Get us up there as fast as you can, partner," Bud said.

"Yes, sir. Will do."

The ride started slowly at first, seeming to hesitate as it was just beginning, but then settled into a smooth, brisk ascent up the natural wonder before us.

We began at about the halfway mark of the tall pines, but were soon cresting their tops, and in a few moments more were looking down at them from high above.

As soon as we cleared them, we could see Daphne again.

She was in the same position, though moving more now, as if trying futilely to scoot back up the mountain.

The cables of the sky ride ran to the left of the Confederate carving, which continued to grow and dominate the right side of our view as we zoomed in closer to the mountain.

We were floating and bouncing as we ascended, the cables providing enough relative slack and tension to cause us to swing slightly as we did.

The large monolith before us was streaked dark gray and etched with grooves that appeared to be the way rain water had snaked its way down from the summit for millions of years.

If he lets her go, I thought, *that's the way her body will descend—along one of the empty riverbed-like troughs already cut into the stone.*

The sheer scope and size of the mountain were staggering,

but its appearance—that of a giant rock hurled into the middle of this relatively flat terrain—was surreal.

"Can anyone get a visual on him?" Frank asked. "Is he behind that lowest rock? I can't see him."

Bud said, "We'll be approaching from the west side. He can't go off the north side, so we just need men approaching from the south and east."

He then began to radio the cops on the south and east sides to get to the top as quickly as they could and not to shoot each other or us as we all approached the same vicinity.

"Wish that damn chopper would get over here," Frank said. "Can this thing go any faster?"

"Sorry," the operator said, shaking his head.

"See how close the others are to the top?" Frank said to Bud.

He did.

"Got runners in each group that should reach the spot about the time we do."

"John, you and Erin take off as soon as we reach the top," Frank said. "Y'all can get over there a lot faster than me and Bud, but . . . be careful. Proceed with caution. Go in with your weapons drawn and ready. We want to save the woman, but . . . don't forget to protect yourselves."

"Yes, sir," I said.

"God, I'd love to be the one to take this fuck down," Erin said.

"You just may get to," Bud said, "but just make sure he doesn't take y'all down with him."

"We've got to make sure that we—" Frank began.

The killer then released Daphne and she slid down the mountain, her free-falling body bouncing and banging off the rock face, scraping off her skin, bashing in her skull, breaking her bones, careening cruelly from one contusion to another. Busting, breaking, splitting, shattering flesh and bone at an astonishing clip, the huge rope trailing behind her like the too-long tail of a doomed, diving kite.

"Oh my God," Frank said.

Erin screamed.

Bud and I gasped.

It took less time than most things I'd see in my lifetime, yet nothing would ever have a greater impact or be more memorable.

"Jesus, did you see that?" someone said into the radio.

"Okay, listen up everybody," Frank said. "There's nothing we can do for her now except catch this sadistic prick, so just concentrate on that. No way he gets off this mountain 'cept in custody."

"Or a body bag," Erin said.

"That one's got my vote," Bud said.

37

As soon as the cable car rocked to a stop and the doors slid open, Erin and I were running—across the platform, through the summit building gift shop and snack bar, out the doors, and around the side.

The top of the mountain was like the surface of the moon, but wet and windy and slippery.

The wind shear was far more powerful than I was prepared for. It slashed at us from every possible angle, buffeting our progress, throwing our every move off balance.

Many of the cracks and crevices and indentations were full of water, and we slipped and tripped and slid and stumbled and splashed as we made our way around to the east side of the mountain.

At first we ran with our weapons drawn, but quickly realized we were going to need our hands free for balance, support, and to catch ourselves when we fell.

We climbed a fence then ran through a small wooded area.

I soon realized there were more wooded areas up here than I had thought.

We ran beneath a radio antenna, the rising sun assaulting our eyes as we moved directly toward it.

The terrain was far more treacherous than I thought it would be, and not just because it was so slick from the dampness, but because of how very many cracks, crevices, rises and indentations were in the granite to trip and fall over or twist an ankle or break a leg.

It was also far more steep than I would have guessed from the ground, the angle and pitch of the elevation more severe as the dome sloped to the edges of the sheer face fall offs.

I stumbled over a slight rise in the rock and fell down.

"You okay?" Erin asked.

"Yeah. Good. Thanks."

I pushed myself up as fast as I could and we continued.

"Wonder which way he'll try to go," she said.

"I'm thinking the east side is too steep," I said. "Not sure the officers from that side are going to be able to make it up from there. Means he probably can't make it down that way either. So my guess is he'll be heading our way or down the south side."

"We need to be ready if he comes this way," she said, "but it's nearly impossible to run with your gun."

"We should probably slow down a bit and pull out our weapons again," I said. "Take a little longer to get there but be safer. Way it is now we could run up on him, and him shoot or stab us before we knew what was happening."

"Probably right but I'd have a hard time convincing my feet to slow down," she said. "I want to get down there and kill that fuck with my bare hands."

We didn't slow down, but I pulled out my weapon anyway. If I fell again, I'd have to hope I could tuck and roll to mitigate the brunt of the blow, or just be prepared to face plant into the hardest, coldest, dampest stone I had ever encountered.

The force of the wind continued to whip at us, its freezing wet tentacles slapping us at every turn.

Erin's radio crackled and she turned it up.

"Where is everyone?" Frank was asking.

"South side team getting close."

"East side team only about halfway up," a voice said. "We'll probably get up there a while after the rest of y'all, but he's not getting by us. We're spread out, so we'll see him if he tries to come down this way, but . . . I doubt he will. It's steep as hell over here."

"Everyone proceed with extreme caution," Frank said. "And be careful where you shoot. There're far more of us up here than him. Careful where you aim. Don't shoot each other."

No longer able to run, we were now crawling and crab walking toward the pile of rocks and stand of trees where the rope holding Daphne had disappeared into.

The sun before us was blinding, but the rock surface beneath our hands remained wet and cold.

I still had my gun out, but it was paying a price—the butt and barrel being scratched and scraped across the hard granite.

"What the hell—" Erin began.

Suddenly, Walt was beside us.

"Where'd you come from?" she said.

"Ran up the west side walking trail," he said. "Y'all ready to get this motherfucker? I say he don't get off this rock alive."

"Let's spread out," I said. "Fifteen to twenty feet apart. Erin, radio the south side team and see how close they are."

She did.

"We're here," the agent said.

"Okay," she said. "Let's fan out, surround the area and slowly close in on it."

"Roger that."

And that's what we all did, eventually reaching the small wooded area.

On the upper side of the topmost boulders the remnants of a small fire still burned beside a one-foot-squared pool of water and drops and smears of blood.

"This is the Stone Mountain Police and the Georgia Bureau of Investigations," Erin yelled. "We have you surrounded. Put down your weapon and walk out with your hands up."

We waited.

My heart was pounding so hard I could hear the ocean in my ears.

Nothing happened.

She then fired a round into the air.

"You can die up here or we can take you into custody and you can tell everyone your side of what happened so they can understand," she said. "It's up to you."

Still nothing.

"Last chance."

When there was still no response, she radioed the others and signaled me and Walt with her hand and we all began slowly walking into the woods, guns out, hammers back, tension high.

The wooded area was like a small pine forest stuck on the side of the mountain, a thin layer of earth on the rock giving life to mostly dormant underbrush and thick fallen pine needles.

The trees weren't nearly as tall as most pines, but high enough to create a canopy that blocked out much of the sun in the area.

I scanned the trees, each one looking like a man standing ready to attack, trying to keep from shooting my fellow task force members or a tree but not wanting to hesitate when I saw the killer.

But there was no sign of the killer.

"He's not here," Erin said into her radio. "East team, any sign of him?"

"We're almost to you and he hasn't come this way."

"Wait," she said. "What is that?"

I followed her gaze to a small clearing in the middle of pines.

There on a tripod was Daphne Littleton's WSB-TV camera, the microphone cord dangling down from it.

We slowly approached it.

Beneath the mic on the ground was a typed note.

Without touching it, she got down on the ground and began to read it as the rest of us gathered around.

Dear Poor Pathetic Cops,

This is the Stone Cold Killer Speaking.

You thought you had me, didn't you?

Sorry not to be here waiting on you when you arrived, but you took so long to get up here that I really just couldn't wait anymore.

Anyway, please don't add insult to injury and be hypocritical about the downfall of Atlanta's most ambitious TV whore. You know you're secretly happy she fell from grace.

So no hard feelings. No harm. No foul. Better luck next time. Try not to be too discouraged. You gave it a good show. You truly did.

You'll have another chance real soon.

Until then.

Yours in blood and stone,

S.C.K.

38

"Where the hell did he go?" Frank said. "How'd he get away?"

His short, going-gray hair was sticking up in the back, his coat looked too small, and the expression on his face was genuine astonishment.

I shook my head and shrugged.

"He's got to still be up here," Bud said, pushing his big black glasses up on his nose. "Hiding somewhere on the mountain."

We were standing inside the summit building, warming up, regathering.

Cops were crawling the mountain, searching for the killer who they believed couldn't have just disappeared into cold, thin air.

The park was still closed, visitors at the inn and campers at the campground sequestered in those areas. The only people on the mountain or out in the park should be cops and the killer.

Two different helicopters were buzzing around, officers with huge binoculars hanging out of them on either side scanning the unforgiving stone for any sign of Daphne's killer.

Frank looked over at me. "What're you thinking?"

"Just trying to figure out how he did it," I said. "And why."

"*Why*?" he said. "What do you mean *why*?"

"Why he broke his pattern," I said. "Daphne wasn't like the other victims. She was fifteen years older, different body type, different personality type. She was taken under different circumstances. She wasn't out running. Wasn't snatched like the others. It's rare for a killer like this to deviate from his series, from his pattern, and when he does there's a reason. I was just trying to figure out the reason."

"We catch him," Bud said, "we can ask him. Doesn't matter *why* as long as we know the *who* and have his ass in custody."

I nodded. "I was thinking the *why* might lead us to the *who*."

Frank nodded. "Let's get Ernestine Campbell back in to go over everything again—including what happened this morning."

"That's all well and good," Bud said, "but we need every available man to be searching for the killer. No way he's off the mountain, let alone out of the park. This is our chance. We're not gonna be able to keep people at the inn and campgrounds for very much longer."

"We approached his position from every angle he could've exited from—"

"Beside a nosedive off the north face," Bud said, "which is what I wish he'd've done."

"How did we miss him?" Frank said. "How did he get by us? Seems impossible."

"Maybe it is," I said.

Frank nodded.

Bud said, "What's that mean?"

"Maybe that's not how he did it," I said. "Maybe he didn't slip through us at all, but got down a different way. We figure that out, we might figure out where he is. We need to look at the tape."

"It could just be her reporting from earlier," Bud said. "No guarantee he recorded anything for us."

"No way he lugged it all the way up there and didn't use it," I said.

"TV station's sending a machine that will play the tape over to the station," Frank said. "Soon as it's processed, we'll take it over and watch it. For now let's go take a look at the body and see what the crime scene techs and the pathologist have to say."

"How long we gonna keep the park closed," Bud asked. "How long we gonna keep people at the inn and the campground?"

Frank frowned and thought about it.

He looked exhausted, but something else too—something deeper, something beyond exhaustion.

"We'll keep the people at the inn and the campground until noon, then only let them exit the park after we check their IDs and vehicles. Park stays closed all day at least. And we search until we find him or run out of daylight. You mind overseeing that?"

"What?" he asked.

"The search and the controlled exit."

"No. Not a problem."

"Let's get our core team together to go to the crime scene," Frank said. "Be best for everyone to hear what is said for themselves. Soon as we finish there, you can use them how you want in the search and the mass exodus."

39

"Body's in bad shape," Gerald Manning was saying. "Mountain really chewed her up."

We were walking in the pine forest near the base of the mountain beneath the east side of the north face.

He had met us and was leading us in.

Unlike the small stand of pines on the mountain we had been in earlier, this was a forest of old growth, tall pines with oak and other hardwoods mixed in.

The sun-dappled ground beneath our feet was damp, the underbrush brown and brittle.

It was colder in the shade of the pines, but they blocked most of the wind.

It was our core team of Frank, Bud, Erin, Walt, Joe, me, two additional GBI agents and Bobby Meredith from the park police, and our breath could still be seen in the frigid early morning air.

"Not much of a crime scene," Gerald was saying. "This is just where she landed. And hell, she hasn't even hit the ground yet, but we're examining the body and the rope."

Frank said, "Whatta you mean she hasn't hit the ground yet?"

"You'll see," he said, then stopped walking and looked back at everyone. "Not used to having this many people walk into my crime scene at one time. I know you're gonna want to get up close and take a good look, but I'm gonna need you to stay back. Nice thing is you don't have to be too careful where you step."

He started walking again and our small group began following again—though more slowly and carefully now.

Soon we reached the crime scene tape and other techs and their equipment.

Ducking beneath it, we continued to the horror beyond.

Daphne Littleton, or what was left of her, hadn't hit the ground yet because she had gotten tangled in the trees.

Suspended some ten feet off the ground, the long rope around her wrists wrapped around other trees and branches, its end dangling some twenty feet from her, her body was twisted sideways but her head was facing down, one open eye staring straight at us.

Her skin was scraped and cut and split, the broken and swollen bones beneath causing her body to be a misshapen mess of odd lumps, deep dents, and unnatural angles.

She had been impaled on at least two branches. Maybe more. It was difficult to discern where what was left of her stopped and the tree branches began.

Dripping blood thudded wetly on the damp dirt beneath her.

"That's the most horrible shit I've ever seen," Walt said.

"Reminds me of traffic accidents I worked back in the day," one of the GBI agents added.

"But this is far worse," Bud said. "It's like she's on display."

"Just the way she would've wanted it," Walt said.

"No one would want this," Erin said.

"She's right," Joe added. "As . . . big time a pain as she was . . . no one should have to . . . go out this way."

I thought about the killer's note. He was wrong. We took no

pleasure in what had befallen this capable and ambitious woman.

"She was so smart and so . . . wary if not wise," Erin said. "How did he get close enough to her to do this?"

"Shit, that's easy," Walt said. "Promised her an exclusive."

"Probably so," Joe said. "Bet that's exactly what it was. *My exclusive interview with the Stone Cold Killer next on WSB-TV news.*"

"What've we got?" Frank said to Gerald.

"Same as before. Some small cuts made with a knife, not life threatening. Have no idea why he does it. Smells of smoke. Ash and soot on her. Tied the same way. Wrists and ankles bound. Long lead rope coming off the binding at the wrists. The rope is big and long but there's nothing extraordinary about it. Thousands of places in the metro area he could've gotten it. Died from blunt force trauma, severe lacerations, hemorrhaging, perforation of major organs, take your pick. Oh, and this time we have what looks like ejaculate on the victim's skin. We'll have to wait for the lab results to be sure, but I'm as sure as I can be at this point."

As they spoke, I walked away from the group to examine the rope, following its looping progression to where its end dangled from a tree branch some twenty feet away.

Besides being long and large, only one feature stood out about it. Though damp from the dew and humidity, toward the end there were four long wet spots approximately two feet in length with a few feet in between them. They were so wet they were still dripping.

Eventually the others joined me.

"Any idea what those are?" I asked Gerald, pointing up at them.

"Not the foggiest," he said.

"If they weren't separated by the space in between 'em I'd say part of the rope spent some time in a small pool of water, but . . ."

"What about four smaller pools of water?" Frank said. "Mountain's full of 'em."

"Could be," Gerald said. "But you'd think when it moved through them, it'd wet the entire area, not leave 'em separated like that."

"I say we get back to searching the mountain and the park so we can ask the son of a bitch when we catch him," Bud said.

40

While the others helped with the search at the park, Frank and I met Ernestine Campbell back at the station to watch the video tape from Daphne Littleton's camera.

"After what happened today," Frank said, "I'm requesting assistance from the FBI. They were extremely helpful with the Wayne Williams investigation and clearly we need help."

I nodded.

Ernie said, "They're the best at cases like this, have the most experience. Will give you the best chance of catching him the quickest."

As usual, Ernie was dressed conservatively, like the clinician and professor she was, but her excitement made her dark face look like that of a little girl's.

We were in the conference room, a tape machine and TV from WSB on the end of the table.

"From the time I make the call, until they send someone and we get them up to speed and they start working the case—it won't be quick. I'd love nothing more than for us to catch him before then. So I'm asking y'all to act as if no one is coming to help, that it's all on us and the clock is ticking. No telling how many lives we can save by solving it sooner rather than later."

We both nodded.

"Y'all want to watch the tape first or—"

"Let's talk a little first," Ernie said. "I think what happened today changes everything, changes how we need to look at this guy and think about him."

"Why's that?"

"It shows incredible flexibility," she said. "He deviated from his pattern enough to include the reporter, but still killed her in largely the same manner. Rarely see something like that."

"Lets us know he's watching the news," I said. "Keeping up with the case that way. We might be able to use that."

"True."

"It rules out Benton Weston," Frank said. "I confirmed he's still out of the country this morning."

"Unless it's a copycat," I said. "He could've paid someone to do it while he was out of the country to deflect suspicion."

"Would explain the differences," Ernie said.

"But the note sounded just the same," Frank said.

"Both could've come from the same copycat," I said.

Ernie nodded. "It *is* possible."

"I'm not saying it's likely or that it's even . . . I'm just saying it's something we need to at least consider. I think it's more likely that the murder of Daphne and the notes are part of the same plan by the killer to appear to be something other than what he is, to make himself look like a thrill killer."

"Instead of . . . what?" Frank said.

"A ritualistic serial killer," I said.

Ernestine raised her eyebrows and nodded approvingly. "And even if it's not a conscious plan on his part, I agree the deviation gives us greater insight into the pattern cases."

I thought about the ritualistic aspects of the first four killings that we knew about and almost had something, but it vanished as quickly as it had come and I couldn't get it back.

"I've been thinking . . ." Ernie said. "We've got to consider that Stone Mountain itself plays a bigger role in what he's doing than maybe we first considered. When I think about the significance of the Klan's history with it and the Confederate carving . . . I think we have to at least consider a radical departure from most previous crimes of this type. Usually serial killers hunt within their one race, but what if because of the racial implications of the mountain it's different this time? What if we have a killer hunting outside of his race? I think it's something that we need to consider. Most serial killers are white and hunt within their own race, but what if this one is black and is hunting outside of his race because of what all has happened on Stone Mountain?"

I nodded and almost had something again.

"Interesting," Frank said.

"I'm just saying it's something to consider," she said. "Let's run it by the FBI profiler that gets assigned to this case."

He nodded. "We will. Anything else before we start the tape? Any ideas how he got away or where he could be hiding?"

"I keep thinking about the note he left us," I said. "'You thought you had me, didn't you?' He knew we'd be coming in and find it, and was confident he'd be gone. How could he be so certain he'd be gone before we got in there and without us seeing him?"

Ernie shook her head. "Absolutely no ideas for you on that."

"Then let's see what's on the tape," Frank said. "You mind starting it, John."

I jumped up and pressed *Play* on the tape machine, the blank blue TV screen replaced with a shot of Daphne holding her mic standing in front of her camera at night.

Her face appeared to be lit by a light on top of the camera, the spill from it revealing she was standing in the woods at night.

I had seen Daphne on TV and in person many, many times. I had never seen her look like this.

Her face was drawn, each line etched more deeply in her pale skin than ever before. Her eyes showed real terror and tears slid down her cheeks intermittently.

It was obvious she was trying not to cry, trying not to act frightened.

"This is Daphne Littleton, WBS-TV Channel 2 News," she said, the mic shaking beneath her quivering chin and soft, wavering voice.

"We were all wrong about the man I labeled the Stone Cold Killer," she said. "I was wrong. I didn't understand what he's doing. None of us did. We were unequal to the task of beholding the brilliance of his work. I humbly ask for forgiveness and I implore you to do the same. This is a marvelous deed being done, wrought by God, worthy of awe and trembling from the bottom of the mountain of the Lord."

It was obvious she was saying what he wanted her to, but if she were reading, I couldn't tell.

When she was finished she stood there for a long, awkward moment, then her eyes grew wide and even more frightened and she began to beg and plead for her life.

And then the recording stopped and the TV screen turned blue again.

Then a few flickers of screams, flashes of horror between blank blue, as if this section of tape had been erased but a shot or two bled through.

Then nothing.

41

The final gasp of day was exhaling its last breath.

Dimness giving way to darkness.

The setting sun streaked the west side of the mountain a dusky harvest orange and cast shadows across the faces of the long-dead Confederate commander, general, and president.

The massive manhunt was over, the cops and search and rescue teams and bloodhounds scattered through the park returning to their vehicles and exiting the park, a weary countenance and dejected expression resting heavily upon them.

"I thought for sure we had him," Bud said.

Frank nodded. "We all did."

"Do you think he's still in the park?" Bud asked. "Are we wrong to call off the search?""My guess is he's long gone, but even if he's not . . . too dangerous to search at night. Especially given how tired everyone is."

We are standing in the small triangle formed by the intersection of Robert E. Lee Boulevard and Jefferson Davis Drive, watching the exodus, waiting on the others.

Walt and Joe pulled up and parked over out of the way.

"Sure as shit thought we had his ass," Walt said. "Can't believe we didn't get him. Smart, crafty son of a bitch, ain't he?"

"He made a new fan today," Joe said.

"I told you about that shit," Walt said. "Cut it out. I'm just impressed. Think about how many people and animals were out here lookin' for his ass today."

"Know y'all are tired," Bud said. "We just want to have a quick word with everyone then you can go."

"We're good," Walt said. "Keep lookin' if you want us to."

"Speak for yourself," Joe said. "I can't take another step."

"Bet your white ass be steppin' toward a cheeseburger 'fore too long."

Joe laughed knowingly.

A white K-9 unit truck from a nearby prison pulled up and two correctional officers parked and got out.

Yelps, barks, and whines came from the dog boxes in the back.

"We thought we had him for sure," the taller of the two men said. "Followed his and the victim's scents all the way up—he used the walkup trail to get up, though more beside it than on it. Got over to the small wooded area like you would imagine. Like we all did. Then he went down toward the quarry on the south side, then back up to where the camera was found, then back down the walking trail. Then either the dogs lost the scent or he was all over the place—really made no sense. Showed him leaving the park then coming back in."

Suddenly the dogs alerted on us and began baying and barking and howling in our direction.

"Are they showing on us?" Bud asked.

"Yeah," the shorter correctional officer said. "Probably picked up on your scent when you were up on the mountain. Been a confusing day for them."

"Let's get 'em home," the taller man said. "Sorry we couldn't be more help. Call us if it happens again and give us a chance to redeem ourselves."

Bud and Frank both thanked them and they joined the parade of other law enforcement vehicles leaving.

Bud looked at the line of cars. "So much manpower . . . and nothing to show for it."

"Wonder if he really left the park and came back in," Frank said.

"What if the dogs weren't confused at all?" I said. "What would it mean if the killer was all over the place? That he left the park and came back?"

Erin arrived with one of the GBI agents and a few minutes later Bobby Meredith arrived with the other.

Erin shook her head as she walked up. "It's not good news," she said.

Frank frowned and shook his head. "I had her pull the receipts from yesterday," he said. "See if any of our three suspects were here."

"They weren't," she said.

"Shit," Bud said. "That puts us back at square one."

"Unless they paid cash," Frank said. "Which at this point you'd expect."

"We need to give their pictures to the people working the gates," Bud said. "Can't believe I didn't think of that sooner."

Frank nodded.

"Unless they paid cash," Erin said, "they weren't here, but guess who was."

"Who?" Bud said. "Dorsey?"

"The rapist Patrick Dorsey," she said. "Made him real uncomfortable to talk to me too."

"Who better than a maintenance man to be all over the place?" Frank said. "And leave and come back in the park as he pleases."

"I don't follow," she said.

Bud explained it to her.

"Oh wow."

"Should we bring him in?" Bud asked.

Frank seemed to think about it. "Tell you what. Why don't Erin and I go back over and talk to him right now—if you're not too tired."

"I'm okay."

"We'll see what he has to say, and I'd like to watch his reaction to you. Depending on how it goes, we can either bring him in or follow up on anything he provides in the way of an alibi."

"Sounds good to me," Erin said. "I just hope it's him and that he runs."

42

I was disappointed that I didn't get to go with Frank and Erin to interview Patrick Dorsey. I was frustrated that we didn't catch the killer today when we had such a great opportunity to. I was exhausted and on edge. Too tired to do anything. Too wired to sleep.

Summer was working the desk. I was in the room alone and missing her, wanting her.

That made me think of Susan, and I felt guilty again for not being able to feel about her the way she did for me.

Going over and sitting on the edge of the bed, I picked up the phone and punched in the number for Scarlett's.

Susan answered.

"Hey," I said.

She hesitated a moment. ". . . Hey."

"How are you?"

"Good. You?" She couldn't have been more coldly polite and emotionless.

"I just called to check on you," I said. "Make sure you were okay. I'm sorry again for how things ended between us. I care very deeply for you and . . ."

"You don't want to be with me right now, right?" she said.

"I . . ."

"Then you're not the one to comfort me or check on me or take care of me. My boyfriend broke my heart. There's really nothing anyone can do about that. But you can only make it worse. Don't be nice. Don't try to give me pastoral care. Don't call me again."

"Okay, but—"

I stopped speaking as she hung up the phone.

I wanted to throw the phone across the room, to kick or hit or break something, but instead I gently replaced the receiver and stood up.

I knew a run would help me feel better, but I just wasn't sure I had the energy to even lace up my shoes.

Then I remembered that a special about Jack the Ripper was airing tonight.

Falling into the bed Summer and I had made love in the night before, I grabbed the remote from the table next to it and clicked on the TV.

As I flipped around to try to find it, I thought about the fact that it had been one hundred years since the Ripper committed his slayings in London's Whitechapel district, and I wondered if one hundred years from now people would still be speculating about who the Stone Cold Killer was.

When I finally found the right channel, John Douglas, the FBI's preeminent profiler, was giving his profile of the UNSUB known as Jack the Ripper, and I wondered if he would be part of the FBI team who worked our case.

As much as I wanted to solve the case myself and do so before the FBI even had time to arrive, I would relish the opportunity to work with and learn from Douglas. He hadn't taught at any of the FBI presentations I had attended, but he was responsible for much of what was taught in them. Ernestine Campbell had met and worked with him but I had not.

The Ripper special was hosted by Peter Ustinov, the English actor who had played Agatha Christie's famous detective Hercule Poirot in a number of made-for-TV movies and most recently in the feature film adaptation of *Appointment with Death*, which I had seen earlier in the year.

It was brave of Douglas to give his profile of Jack the Ripper on national TV. It couldn't necessarily be proven or disproven, of course, but it could be ridiculed—especially by the legions of law enforcement that believed criminal profiling was about a half step up from psychics and fortunetellers.

Among other things, Douglas said that the killer was mentally unstable, a loner, someone who wasn't out of place in the Whitechapel district. He went on to say that the UNSUB would have suffered from delusions of persecution, unwarranted jealousies, and exaggerated self-importance, and that he would be sexually dysfunctional since there was no evidence of sexual assault or sadistic torture. He said the Ripper hated and was afraid of women, and that removing their sexual and reproductive organs postmortem was an attempt to take their sexual power, to essentially neuter them.

It was a fascinating profile and made me think about the UNSUB we were after.

In what ways is he like the Ripper? How is he different?

I was thinking I was beginning to see some similarities and some differences.

The Ripper was frenzied in his attacks and murders. The Stone Cold Killer was not. He was careful and controlled.

The Ripper was blunt and brutal and messy. The Stone Cold Killer was precise and clean and his manner of murder was hands off, even indirect and bloodless on his end.

Both the Ripper and the Stone Cold Killer had major issues with women, their power, their sexuality, and though they responded differently to the fear and paranoia and threat they felt, I believed they in some ways had the same motivation.

As much as Douglas's profile of the Ripper was helpful and inspiring, it was another segment of the show that gave me the next piece of the puzzle.

It had to do with the killer's name—Jack the Ripper.

The two names originally used for the UNSUB were the Whitechapel Murderer and Leather Apron.

Jack the Ripper came later in the form of a letter penned by someone claiming to be the murderer. The letter was distributed to the papers, and the name stuck. One hundred years later he was still being called by it. But the letter wasn't written by the murderer. It was written by someone as a sadistic sort of joke, or more likely, a member of the media attempting to intensify interest in the case and the number of newspapers sold.

And then it hit me.

Though I didn't expect to get him, I called Frank at home.

To my surprise he answered.

"I figured you'd still be talking to Dorsey," I said.

"Then why'd you call?"

"Couldn't help myself. Have an idea. How'd it go with Dorsey?"

"We couldn't find him. Wasn't in the park or at his home. We'll try again tomorrow. Whatcha got? I only have a second."

"You got a handwriting analyst?"

"Of course."

"I think we need to compare the writing of the letter we got with samples of Daphne Littleton's," I said. "I think she wrote it so she could gin up interest in the story and name the killer herself. I think that's why he killed her. I think he made her write the note we found under her microphone. That's why what was written doesn't fit what the killer's doing."

"I'll get it checked out as soon as I can. See you in the morning."

43

"Hey," Summer said.

I had just walked into the empty lobby from the back door.

"Hey."

"I figured you'd be out by now," she said as she shuffled papers behind the counter.

As I got closer I saw what the papers were. She had one of my file folders from the case with several pages of notes, witness statements, crime scene photos, and autopsy results in it.

"What're you—"

"Hope you don't mind," she said. "Figured you'd be sleeping and not need them tonight. I was trying to see if I could pick up something, if some detail or statement or something would spark a connection for me so I could help you catch him."

"Wish you would've asked."

"I meant to."

"If anyone sees you with those I'll be thrown off the case," I said.

"Oh, shit. Sorry. I—here, take it back. I'm—I had no idea. Was just trying to help. I would never . . ."

She handed me the file.

"Did you pick up anything?" I asked.

She shook her head. "Had just started to look at it. Why're you up?"

"Couldn't fall asleep."

"I could help with that if I wasn't stuck behind this . . ."

I smiled and could feel myself getting erect as memories of our lovemaking from the night before floated through my mind.

"How quick can you be? I could leave a note on the counter like I do when I go to the bathroom."

I smiled. "Quick would not be a problem."

She gave me a warm smile of her own, withdrew a *Be Back in 5* note from beneath the desk, and placed it on the check-in countertop next to the bell.

She disappeared through a door to her right and reappeared next to me on this side of the desk a few moments later.

Taking my hand, she led me up the large, curving staircase.

"I've never made love to a woman in uniform before," I said.

"You're gonna like it," she said. "But don't get too used to it. This is a temporary gig. Soon as we catch the madman I'm retiring this thing."

"Then I better make the most of it while I can."

The second floor restaurant was dark and empty.

"Are you sure no one's up here?" I asked.

"Positive. Besides, what's the worst that could happen? We get caught? Embarrassed? Or I lose a job I'm only doing to—"

"You had me at *positive*."

She let out a young girl's giggle.

We weaved around the round tables and chairs to a set of French doors that led out onto the balcony.

In the moonlight streaming in through the little panes of glass and the spill from the lamps in the parking lot, she lifted her uniform skirt and shimmied out of her panties.

It was sexy and seductive and sweet.

She then unbuttoned her blouse, unhooked her bra, and pulling her coat and shirt back and her bra up, exposed her beautiful bare breasts.

Taking my hands she guided them up and placed them on the warm skin of her erect nipples.

She then began to unbutton and unzip my jeans as we kissed.

Eventually, she eased down on the floor before me, pulling up her skirt and opening her coat and blouse again.

"Sorry we don't have time for more," she said.

"I'm so grateful for this," I said, kneeling down between her legs and sliding into her.

There was something enormously erotic about her still being partially clothed, hiking up the skirt of her work uniform and opening her hotel blouse and blazer.

It was the first time I had made love to a clothed woman. There was something about it that made her unclothed parts, the flashes of pale flesh, seem all the more naked, all the more exposed.

It was also the first time I had made love in a public place, and I found the experience equal parts exciting and anxiety inducing.

But she felt so good, so like the embodiment of serenity, and soon I wasn't aware of our surroundings or worried about someone catching us.

We made love in the small rectangles of moonlight, the silent, magnificent mountain our only witness.

Afterward, as we were lying in each other's arms, looking up at the mountain, she said, "I'd like us to make love up on top of it someday."

I nodded as I thought about it.

She added, "Just picture bending me over a boulder, pulling down my panties, hiking up my skirt. Up that high, that much closer to God. It's got a pure, sacred energy, an ancient magic. It's a holy place. Nothing he can do can change that."

And then I saw it, got a better glimpse of what I had been struggling to make out before.

"What is it?" she said. "Where are you going?"

44

After thanking her for the amazing experience and the flash of inspiration, I walked Summer back down to the front desk, kissed her, then ran out of the lobby and back to our room with the file folder.

Something she had said had ignited a piece of kindling in me and fired up connections with other thoughts, ideas, inspirations hovering at the fringes of my mind.

Summer had said that the mountain was sacred, that to be on the top of it was to be closer to God, and that had been the reminder I needed to make the other blurry images come into focus.

Now I knew, or thought I did, why there was no rape or sexual assault—except of Daphne—why there was no torture or pre or post-mortem mutilation. I knew why he cleaned and washed them, why he cut them, and why he built a fire.

He was offering sacrifices.

He was climbing to the mountain top to present his offerings to God like so many had done before him.

That was why there had to be a fire, had to be the shedding of blood, had to be a cleansing.

It was why I had been thinking of the word ritual when I thought about what he was doing. He wasn't a thrill killer. He was a ritualistic killer who saw himself as a man of God making sacrifices for his and their sins.

Most of my things, including my Bible, were still in the old farmhouse on Flakes Mill Road, but I knew there would be a Bible in the bedside table in our room.

I rushed in and flipped through the first book in it until I found the story of Abraham offering his only son on an altar on Mount Moriah in Genesis 22:1-19.

Running my finger across and down the page I read the passage.

1 *Some time later God tested Abraham. He said to him, "Abraham!"*

"Here I am," he replied.

2 Then God said, "Take your son, your only son, whom you love—Isaac—and go to the region of Moriah. Sacrifice him there as a burnt offering on a mountain I will show you."

3 Early the next morning Abraham got up and loaded his donkey. He took with him two of his servants and his son Isaac. When he had cut enough wood for the burnt offering, he set out for the place God had told him about. 4 On the third day Abraham looked up and saw the place in the distance. 5 He said to his servants, "Stay here with the donkey while I and the boy go over there. We will worship and then we will come back to you."

6 Abraham took the wood for the burnt offering and placed it on his son Isaac, and he himself carried the fire and the knife. As the two of them went on together,7 Isaac spoke up and said to his father Abraham, "Father?"

"Yes, my son?" Abraham replied.

"The fire and wood are here," Isaac said, "but where is the lamb for the burnt offering?"

8 Abraham answered, "God himself will provide the lamb for the burnt offering, my son." And the two of them went on together.

9 When they reached the place God had told him about, Abraham built an altar there and arranged the wood on it. He bound his son Isaac and laid him on the altar, on top of the wood. 10 Then he reached out his hand and took the knife to slay his son. 11 But the angel of the Lord called out to him from heaven, "Abraham! Abraham!"

"Here I am," he replied.

12 "Do not lay a hand on the boy," he said. "Do not do anything to him. Now I know that you fear God, because you have not withheld from me your son, your only son."

13 Abraham looked up and there in a thicket he saw a ram caught by its horns. He went over and took the ram and sacrificed it as a burnt offering instead of his son. 14 So Abraham called that place The Lord Will Provide. And to this day it is said, "On the mountain of the Lord it will be provided."

15 The angel of the Lord called to Abraham from heaven a second time 16 and said, "I swear by myself, declares the Lord, that because you have done this and have not withheld your son, your only son, 17 I will surely bless you and make your descendants as numerous as the stars in the sky and as the sand on the seashore. Your descendants will take possession of the cities of their enemies,18 and through your offspring all nations on earth will be blessed, because you have obeyed me."

The brutality and barbarism of both humans and animal sacrifice was almost as ancient as humanity itself.

For the adherents of the world's many and diverse religions the concepts of sacrifice—both animal and human—have a sheen of acceptability and even orthodoxy, particularly when seen as historic events in the evolution of the understanding of the divine and the divine-human relationship.

Indoctrinated from an early age, they are told these things

were required to appease the gods or the God and they read them in the pages of texts they are told are sacred and even God-inspired.

It wasn't difficult to imagine a mentally-ill psychopath justifying his murder of young women by claiming that what he was doing was offering sacrifices to please the Lord—just like Abraham, Moses and Aaron, Samuel and David.

I had heard sermons preached and read articles encouraging people to lay down what they held dear on Mount Moriah, to give to God their best and most precious gifts as offerings acceptable in the sight of the Lord.

Is that what you're doing? Is that why you don't rape them? Why you take them up there, build a fire and bind them? Is Stone Mountain your Mount Moriah? Are these young women your Isaacs? Are you offering sacrifices to God? For their sin or yours? Or are you offering them in an attempt not to sin, so remove the temptation altogether?

45

"While the rest of us were sleepin' last night," Frank said, "John was working his ass off on the case and having some major breakthroughs."

Our core group plus a few extra GBI agents and park police were gathered in the small conference room.

Though Frank looked the worst, everyone looked weary and dejected.

"First," he said, "he theorized that the letter we received was written and sent not by the killer but the reporter and most recent victim, Daphne Littleton."

"Was it?" Walt asked. "Did that . . . write a fake letter and . . ."

"We're gathering samples of her handwriting now," Frank said, "but her camera man already made a statement this morning saying she did in fact write the letter."

Frank paused for a moment as most everyone in the room reacted audibly to the revelation.

"That means she gave him the name Stone Cold Killer," he said. "It means none of the words in the letter were his. Meaning . . . we have to rethink how we view the killer, what he's doing, how we catch him."

"What about the note?" Joe asked. "She write that too?"

"The note found under her microphone on the mountain does appear to be written by her, though I'm not so sure he didn't tell her at least some of what to say. Just don't know. We'll have it analyzed—and not just the handwriting itself. He may have had her actually write it but told her some of what to say."

Erin looked at me. "That's why the thrill kill thing didn't match up with what he was actually doing, right?"

I nodded.

"Which leads to the next thing John came up with last night," he said.

"Wait just a second," Bud said, clearing his throat and adjusting his glasses. "Before you . . . get to that. Sorry, but . . . we need to take a closer look at the Littleton woman's camera man. What's his name?"

"Stan," Walt said. "Stan the Camera Man."

"He's always with her," Bud said. "They're inseparable—hell, he even knows she's the one who wrote the letter—but he's not with her when she goes to meet with the killer? Have a hard time buying that."

Frank was nodding. "You're exactly right," he said. "Good thinking. Who wants to—"

"I got it," Walt said. "Let you know what I find out."

"Okay," Frank said. "Back to John's theory of what the killer is actually doing. John, why don't you explain?"

I did.

I walked them through some concepts of sacrifice and what was involved—mountains, fire, water, the shedding of blood—shared with them the story of Abraham.

"It's just a theory," I said, "but—"

"It fits," Bud said. "I think you're right."

"Thing about killers like this one," Frank said, "is . . . nothing's gonna fit exactly. They're not completely consistent and certainly not motivated by rational thought, but . . . yeah I think it's accurate. I think it should be our working theory."

"If it's right," I said. "If any of it is . . . it gives us insight into the killer—what he's doing and why. Hopefully something about that will help us catch him."

Erin's eyes widened and her mouth fell open. "So," she said, "let's tie this to an actual suspect. What if a rapist—someone like Patrick Dorsey, say—was trying not to rape women anymore. So instead of raping them . . . he offers them to God as some sort of sacrifice."

I nodded. "That's good. He could blame them for what he has done in the past. Blame the victim. So he sees killing them as punishment for their sin. Or . . . as in the case of Abraham . . . he wants them so badly . . . wants to possess and use, control and dominate them . . . that he sees what he's doing as offering up—actually sacrificing—what he most wants, his best gift."

"Damn," Walt said. "That's some deep shit. What the hell kinda cop are you?"

Erin said, "A smart one."

Frank said, "The fact that we found traces of semen on Daphne could prove what we're saying. With her the killer slipped up and sinned again."

"Yeah," Walt said, "shot his sin all over her."

Ignoring him, Frank said, "Something he could've been doing all along and just washing it off or . . ."

"Because she was different than the others," I said, "he didn't feel the same about her. She wasn't one of his pattern sacrifices, so he wouldn't see it as sinning—or at least not as bad because of who she was. Or what she wasn't."

"We're gonna bring Patrick Dorsey in for questioning today," Frank said.

"If we can find his ass," Walt said. "Might be in Mexico by now."

"We've decided to forego the casual conversation at his home or job approach and bring him in for a formal interview. And we're gonna let Erin conduct it. See how he reacts to having a woman do it."

"That should be interesting," Joe said.

"Final thing," Frank said. "FBI is sending someone from their Atlanta field office tomorrow. Starting then they will be assisting in this investigation. Few things we all need to remember. They're assisting, not taking over the investigation. They'll be working with us. They will be an asset and can really help us. Welcome them and help them. But the thing is . . . it won't be quick. It will take a little while for them to assign agents and for them to get up to speed on the case and really start working it with us. And that leads me to my most important point. Work this case like we're solely and ultimately responsible for it. Because we are. The FBI isn't going to come in and solve it for us or catch the killer. We have to do it with their help, but I'd rather do it sooner than that. I'd rather us do it before they're even up and running—and not because it'll make us look competent and it's our job, but because it will save lives. So act like today is the last day you have to solve this case and save the life of someone you care deeply about, okay?"

46

"Do I make you nervous, Pat?" Erin asked.

He shook his small head. "No, ma'am, you don't. And it's Patrick."

Patrick not Pat Dorsey was far more put together than the last time we had seen him. His thin, sun-damaged face was clean shaven, the fine gray hair of his long ponytail looked to have been recently shampooed and blow-dried.

He and Erin were sitting across from each other on opposite sides of the table in the interview room. Audio and video tapes were rolling and Frank, Bud, Ernestine, and I were observing through a two-way mirror in the recording room.

Walt and Joe were chasing down other leads relating to Benton Weston, Randy North, and Teddy Sears.

"Patrick, sorry," Erin said. "Women don't make you nervous?"

He shrugged. "I guess, maybe. I don't know. I like women. I . . . ain't claiming to understand them or anything, but . . ."

"I hear ya," she said. "Well, fair enough. Thanks again for coming in to talk to us. We appreciate it. Just trying to figure a few things out, tie up a few loose ends. That sort of thing. For the tape and to remind you again . . . you're not under arrest and are free to go anytime you want. It would look bad . . . be more suspicious and cause us to take a closer look at you, but . . . you can do it."

He nodded. "Don't mind answerin' questions. Got nothing to hide, man. My hands and conscience are clean."

"We appreciate that. Now, we looked into the story you gave us about your previous troubles and we're getting some conflicting information. You said your accuser was your wife's best friend, but . . . it looks like they were at most merely acquaintances."

"They were friends. I shouldn't have fucked her, but . . . it was . . . what's the word everybody's using now . . . consensual. We fooled around. She came twice. It was a mutual thing, man. We both wanted it—her more than me. I was wrong to cheat, but I didn't rape her."

"Okay," Erin said. "As far as the assault . . . You said you were just defending yourself when your wife and her friend jumped you—"

"Yeah?"

"But their injuries . . . they both took a pretty brutal beating. Broken collarbone. Dislocated jaw. Fractures. Contusions."

"They were on something . . . wouldn't stop coming at me with knives and a fire poker and a baseball bat. Maybe I was a little too . . . ah . . . We were all coked up. They attacked me. I didn't attack them. I defended myself, man. That's it. And the truth of it is . . . I was never convicted of anything. So this is just hearsay, man."

"No, it's not hearsay, but . . . we'll move on from that for now."

"Good, 'cause I thought this was about the mountain murders, man. I mean . . . come on. Nobody wants to sit here and have their past drugged up."

"You were in the park every day there was a murder."

"So were a lot of people. I work there. A whole bunch of us do."

"Speaking of . . . you applied to the Stone Mountain Park police, didn't you?"

"Yeah?"

"Have you applied to other law enforcement agencies before?"

He shrugged. "A few, yeah."

"Ever been a cop?"

He shook his head. "Never worked out."

"Why?"

"Just different stuff. No one thing. I don't stay in one place for very long. Lot easier just getting a construction or maintenance job."

"But you're interested in law enforcement," she said.

"Sure, I guess," he said, pursing his lips and shrugging.

"If you were us how would you go about catching him?"

"Who? The killer? Got no idea, man. Maybe . . . I don't know . . . just like set a trap or something. 'Course . . . he keeps targeting cunts like that reporter bitch . . . you might not want to catch him just yet."

Erin hesitated a moment, then said, "Good point. Any other, ah, women you have in mind?"

"Not off the top of my head, but I could make a list and get back with you."

"Please," she said. "I'd love to see it."

He nodded and scratched the side of his face with a thumbnail. "You got it."

"Would I be on it?"

"Not so far," he said. "But we're not done yet, are we?"

"No, we're not. Fair point. Did you know any of the victims?"

He paused for a moment. His eyes widened and he looked caught or trapped or surprised. But it was just for a moment then he shook his head.

"Didn't know any of them?" she said. "You sure?"

"Positive. Never even saw any of 'em before 'cept the reporter —and that was just on TV."

"You sure you didn't know Pam Nichols, the second victim?"

"Absolutely positive. Didn't know her. Never met her."

Erin nodded. "I believe you. You didn't know her, did you?"

"I honestly didn't," he said shaking his head.

Erin continued to nod as she withdrew an eight by ten color photo from a file folder on the desk next her and slid it over in front of him. "I believe you, which is why it really makes me wonder why you went to her funeral—something killers sometimes do."

47

"What do y'all think?" Frank asked.

Erin had joined us in the observation recording room. Patrick was still seated in the interview room.

Ernestine nodded. "He could be our guy. Need to know more about him. But it fits for him to be doing menial, hired help labor. The question is . . . is he smarter than he's coming across?"

Erin nodded. "He definitely is. What we're getting is an act. He's playing Hippy Hank laid-back dude, but you heard some of those toxic leaks. Calling women cunts and bitches and he was glad the reporter was dead."

Frank nodded. "I agree."

Ernestine said, "We need to know more about him. See if we can track down info about the other places he's lived. Moving around like he has may be how he's eluded detection so far. See if any other similar crimes have been committed in those places. Also, we need to know if he's had any recent stressors. What set him off, triggered him this time? A breakup? The death of someone close to him? Did he lose another job just before getting this one? That kind of thing."

"He's pretty slight," I said. "Seems weak and out of shape.

Smelled like he smokes. Would he be fast enough to catch the victims? Would be strong enough to control them? Get them and the other things up the mountain?"

"It's a good question," Frank said.

"Following the pattern of the Bible story you shared with us," Erin said, "he'd make them carry the wood and supplies up the mountain, right?"

I nodded. "Yeah. Isaac carrying the wood up the mountain is believed by some to be a metaphor for Christ carrying his own cross. The whole thing is seen as the story of Christ—being sacrificed by his father for the salvation of the world. Maybe he's following that pattern and metaphor. But he'd have to control them enough to get them to do that."

"We agree he's the best suspect we have right now, right?" Frank said.

"If Benton Weston is still really out of the country and Daphne's murder wasn't the work of a copycat," Ernestine said.

"I know we're short on manpower," Bud said, "but I think we need to put a tail on him."

"I agree," Frank said. "We'll just have to figure out how."

"So for now we're gonna cut him lose?" Erin said.

Frank nodded.

"Thank him for his cooperation and reassure him we don't think he's involved. Make him think we don't consider him a suspect."

48

"Are you getting attached to me?" Summer asked.

We had just made love and were still lying in bed, which was where I intended to stay when she went to work in a few minutes.

I smiled. "Just might be."

"Does our age difference bother you?" she asked.

I shook my head. "Not at all."

"Do you think I'm a surrogate for your mom?" she asked.

"I'd rather not think about that," I said. "Particularly in light of what we just did."

"I'm serious."

"Would it matter if you were?" I asked.

"I care so deeply for you, John. You're a truly remarkable young man. And I just don't want to do anything that would . . . that wouldn't be good for you."

I started to ask her if I were a surrogate for her son who died but decided I shouldn't, that I probably was, and that it was okay that I was.

"Are you telling me not to get attached to you?" I asked.

"I'm not sure what I'm saying exactly. Just felt like I should bring it up."

I thought about it for a long moment. Finally I said, "Everything is good right now, right?"

"Very," she said. "The best."

"And any issue we might have—with our age difference or being in different stages of our lives or that we might eventually go in different directions—all has to do with the future, right?"

"Right."

"Then why don't we both spend some time contemplating it and revisit it sometime soon—like maybe after this case is over—but in the meantime keep loving and caring for each other the best we can and not borrow any trouble from tomorrow, from the future and what might happen."

She leaned over and kissed me. "I like that plan," she said. "I like it a lot. You're wise beyond your years. No wonder I love you the way I do."

My eyes widened a bit.

"Did I say that out loud?" she said. "It's true. I do love you. I have since we first met at the missing and murdered kids group last year. Broke my heart when things ended between us the way they did. I guess the truth is . . . *I'm* getting attached to *you*. That's my . . . that's probably the real reason I brought it up. I mean I was genuinely asking about you and I care about how all this affects you. I don't want to see you get hurt. And I'm not really all that concerned about me. I'm really not. Nothing can happen to me any worse than already has. But I'm sure what's why I even brought it up . . . was because of how attached I'm becoming. Am I scaring you yet?"

"Not at all," I said, and pulled her to me and held her, our naked bodies pressing hard against each other. "Not at all."

"Are you sure?"

"Positive."

"Good. I can let you go when you're ready to. I've done it before. It's going to all be okay."

"Yes it is," I said.

"Do you want to make love again before I have to get ready for work?"

"Is that some sort of trick question?"

49

He had been watching her for a while.

She still had no idea.

He wanted her.

Wanted to possess her. Control her. Take her. Make her his own. Dominate. Subjugate.

He wanted her, but he couldn't have her.

It was a sin. It was against God. Her body was the very entryway to hell itself. To enter her would be to enter hell.

His mom had taught him that. Taught him so many things with a Bible in one hand and a rod in the other.

At times it was an actual rod, at others it was an old leather belt, a piece of oak firewood, a dull pair of kitchen scissors, an extension cord, a wire coat hanger, a rusted pocket knife her daddy had used on her, and the sharp end of an old metal fan blade.

Spare the rod and spoil the child. Says so right there in God's word. Just like *For whom the Lord loves He chastens, And scourges every son whom He receives.*

The Lord God had chastened and scourged him by his mother's firm hand. She had made sure he was worthy to be received.

The devil wanted him, but his mother wouldn't allow that—even if she had to offer him as a sacred sacrifice to God. Instead she chastened him, scourged him, taught him the sacred art of self-scourging and ultimately how to make sacrifices out of those whose bodies would destroy him, would fling him into the lake of fire for eternal torture and torment.

By offering them up as a sin offering to God, he was not only saving himself but all the other poor souls they would deliver to Satan.

He was weak and he knew it. He had sinned with the reporter, had given into the lust of the flesh. He hadn't put it inside her, but he had sinned, had gotten carnal with her. She was filthy and deserved what she got, but he had to be careful.

He'd have to be especially careful with the wicked woman child he was following now.

She thought she was smart, this little daughter of the great whore of Babylon. She had stopped running at the park. But she had not stopped running, had not stopped shaking and bouncing the shame of her sin up and down the street for every weak and struggling child of God to see, to look upon with the lust of the eyes, which of course leads to the lust of the flesh.

Instead of running in the park, she was running in the town of Stone Mountain—where even more sinners could see her.

You can run but you can't hide—not from the eyes of the Lord that roam to and fro searching for sinners, searching for sin.

She was wearing even less than she did when she ran in the park.

He wanted to punish her, wanted to hurt her for her shame, but he knew that was for God to do.

God will do the judging and punishing, he alone is worthy to pass the sentence. You just make the offering.

You're the priest. You offer the sacrifice. Everything else is up to God.

You can and should enjoy making the sacrifice. Nothing wrong with that. But wrath and vengeance belong to the Lord.

He was wearing his human suit, which would make this easier.

He had done it both ways—snatched the sacrifices with and without his human suit, his mask of sanity—and each had its advantages and he liked it both ways, but there was no question that his human suit made it easier.

He wouldn't get to chase her like he would if they were in the park late at night, which was a pity. He loved the chase. Loved seeing their muscular bodies run for their lives, but that wasn't to be this time. This time was just going to be easy.

So much easier. She actually smiled and looked relieved as he approached her.

Little lamb to the slaughter. Come here little lamb. Come to the shepherd of your annihilation.

She stumbled up the mountain carrying the wood for her own sacrificial fire.

It was amazing what he could get them to do, pathetic how hard they worked to prolong their meaningless little existences. Even now, knowing what was coming, they still preferred to make the trek up the mountain to be dropped off it rather than take a bullet to the head down below it.

He was reminded of all the things his mother was able to get his brother to do to avoid the beatings, the humiliation, the pain, yet somehow he had to know he was going to get all those things anyway. All he did was prolong them, make them worse, get hours of her taunts and touches before getting the torture.

Eventually, she had made a sacrifice of his brother and turned all her attention onto him. But he had learned from his brother's mistakes and he was ready. Or at least far more prepared than he would have been.

She still got the best of him plenty, but not nearly as much as she would have otherwise.

She used to place his penis between the sharp ends of a pair of kitchen scissors and make him stand there and quote scripture. As he did, she would turn on porn and threaten to *slice it off* if he got an erection.

He never did.

Still doesn't.

Eventually he not only outgrew her physically but mentally, emotionally, and spiritually as well. He consistently bested her in every way.

It was then that she decided to sacrifice him to God, but she had waited too long. She was no match for him and he instead made a sacrifice of her.

But before she went the way of all flesh she had taught him a lot—including how to appear human, how to mimic everyone else, how to wear a mask and play a part. And he had learned it well, but he hadn't stopped there. He had added to it, built on it, perfected it, until he had arrived at what he was today—an unstoppable force hidden in plain sight, a predator whose unsuspecting prey welcomes and, at times, actually comes to him.

After he had built the fire to attract the attention of God to his offering, he bound her, cut her, for there is no remission of sins without the shedding of blood, he laid his hands on her to transfer his sin to her, then he shoved her off the mountain as a sin offering to the Lord.

She sped down the mountain with astounding velocity, bouncing and rolling, sliding and careening until she hit the top of Robert E. Lee's head, slid down his nose and the lapel of his coat until she came to rest in the crook of his bent right elbow.

He hadn't realized he was so directly above the enormous

Confederate carving, but of course with a surface of over an acre and a half, it took up a lot of room.

Recessed some forty-two feet into the side of the solid stone mountain, the world's largest bas-relief would of course be the place where any falling object would fall into.

He should have realized that before now. If he had, and if he had let his other offerings go around this same spot and placed them all within the huge crooks and crevices of the carving no one would yet know what he was doing and he would still be able to worship God and offer his sacrifices out of the sight of the ignorant, the unrepentant, and the unregenerate.

For when you pray, do not as the hypocrites do in public in order to be seen and heard, but pray to God in secret. Don't let your left hand know what your right hand is doing.

He wasn't sure how long this new hiding place could go undetected—especially since so many were already watching the mountain—but he'd be grateful for every second that his sacred sacrifice was just between him and God.

50

For the next few days, we made very little forward progress on the case.

A lot was happening—the arrival of the FBI, the difficult and time-consuming work of getting them briefed on everything that had happened so far, the surveillance of Patrick Dorsey, the following up of tips and leads, the continued investigations into Benton Weston, Randy North, and Teddy Sears, and the sting operation that had Erin out running around the mountain each night and a rotating group of us following her.

Activity. Movement. No forward progress.

It was early evening on a particularly cold night in early November. I had a couple of hours before I had to go out and follow Erin around in the dark park, hoping the madman would jump out of the dormant brown brush and attack her.

While I waited, I sat in the lobby of the Stone Mountain Inn and worked on the case.

I was in the lobby because Summer was working and I wanted to be close to her and because I had spent too much time alone in the empty hotel room lately.

Guests came and went—checking in, checking out the paintings hanging in the wide, curving stairwell, asking for various things—directions, extra towels, additional linens—or to complain about an odor or the discomfort or dirtiness of their room.

In between, we talked and flirted and even kissed, but it was way too early in the evening for a trip up the staircase for a quickie on the floor by the french doors. I did, however, remain hopeful that perhaps when my sting operation had concluded later tonight we might be able to.

I found Summer irresistible, my desire for her insatiable, and the longer I was with her the deeper I was falling for her.

She was so cute in her little hotel uniform and blazer, and I couldn't look at it without remembering the times she had taken it off for me or at least opened it to expose the parts of her I was most trying to gain access to.

Nothing about her seemed forty-something—not her energy or body or demeanor or dress. She was the perpetual mature teenage girl quickly becoming the girl of my dreams, and the more time I spent with her the more Jordan Moore began to ever so slightly fade, her grasp on me ever so slightly loosen.

Summer and I had spent a lot of time together lately, and during all that time I had only discovered a few annoyances—one of which she was doing right now.

During and especially after drinking a drink—sweet tea, Coke, Sprite, whatever—she chomped on her ice with an enthusiasm and aggression like I had never quite seen before. The closest thing I could compare it to was the way some moviegoers chewed on popcorn once the lights went down.

As I attempted to roll the case around in my mind I found what she was doing with her ice distracting and irritating.

I continued to shake up the various elements of the case like dice in a cup, rolling them around and letting them tumble out in different combinations.

The rope. What about the rope?

The victims. Have we missed anything they have in common?

How is he choosing them? Why does he go for this type?

How did he get off the mountain when we had it surrounded?

Why does he sacrifice them? How did that particular psychopathology develop?

What does he do with their things—their clothes, shoes, purses, jewelry?

All the while Summer, in between helping guests and answering the phone, chomp, chomp, chomping on ice.

Why was the rope wet in certain spots? From what?

Am I wrong about him making sacrifices? If so, what's he doing?

Who are you? What do you look like? What mask are you hiding behind?

I thought through everything Benton Weston and Patrick Dorsey said during their interviews.

"Could you do that a little quieter, please?" I asked.

"What?" Summer said, totally unaware of what I was referring to.

"Chomping on the ice," I said. "I don't see how you haven't broken a molar by now."

"Sorry. Didn't realize I was doing it. Was it loud?"

"Just a little. Thank you."

"You getting anywhere?"

I shook my head. "No. Not—"

And then—*lightning bolt.*

"What is it?" she said. "You've figured something out, haven't you?"

All of sudden, when I was thinking about something else, a moment of clarity and vision, the possibility of an insight.

The rope. The large, intermittent wet spots near the top of it.

I wasn't sure if it was correct or not, but I saw a solution, an explanation as clearly and vividly as I saw Summer's smile when she realized that she had been chomping ice loudly without realizing it.

Large blocks of ice frozen around the top of the rope, hooked around the rocks and trees, melting as the day broke and the temperature rose, causing Daphne to plunge to her death.

Is it really possible? How would he do it? How would he get the rope and blocks of ice to the top of the mountain?

If I was right about it, it would explain why we didn't catch him even though we thought we had him surrounded. He was long gone by the time we were even aware Daphne was up there.

"Tell me," she said.

I jumped up. "I'll tell you when I get back tonight, but whatever you do . . . don't ever stop eating ice. For the rest of your life chomp it just as loudly as you like."

51

There was a lot of chatter and activity on our radios tonight—more overlap between the surveillance of Patrick Dorsey and the sting operation involving Erin running than we had ever had before.

"He's moving again," Joe said.

"Got 'im," Walt said.

They had followed Dorsey from his house to a little restaurant in the town of Stone Mountain where he had eaten alone and now he was on the move again—presumably back home.

"Must be a special night," Joe said. "All this time of followin' him . . . never seen him eat out at a restaurant. Not once."

Frank and I were following Erin as she ran along the south side of the mountain near the old quarry.

It was just the two of us following her and I was uncomfortable with us being in the same vehicle, but I was happy for the chance to ask him about Sylvia and tell him about my theory about the ice blocks.

"How would he get them and the girls and all the other stuff up the mountain?" he said.

"I've been thinking about that," I said. "He could be driving up. There's an old service road. They used it when they carved the monument and when they built the summit building. Still use it. One of the park police told me as long as it wasn't wet he could have an ambulance to the top of the mountain in eight minutes."

"And if it's raining?"

"It's too slick and slippery to use at all. No traction."

"It was wet the morning Daphne died," he said.

"Maybe he did it before it rained. But he could also be using a wheelbarrow or some other cart or even a small vehicle—a motorcycle maybe."

He seemed to think about it for a moment. "No one would question a maintenance man on a vehicle or with a wheelbarrow."

I nodded. "The other thought I had is that he's making two trips," I said. "He takes all or some of the supplies up and leaves them hidden, then comes back down to get his victim."

"It was cold enough that the blocks of ice wouldn't melt much while they sat up there and waited for him to return."

It was dark and cold and Erin seemed to be jogging more slowly than in the past, her movements more stiff, less fluid, and I was sure she was just as exhausted as the rest of us—and far more physically fatigued.

"We should probably make it an early night," I said. "Erin looks exhausted."

"Yeah," he said. "We could all do with a little extra sleep."

The radio was turned down some, but Joe and Walt had been talking on it in the background during our entire conversation. Now Joe was saying, "Looks like he's headed back home."

"Roger that," Walt said. "You got him if he turns off Main Street. I'll keep driving straight and circle around."

"We've had some other developments," Frank said. "Quite a few. Not sure what they all mean, but I'd like us to meet with

Ernestine and the FBI agent in charge tomorrow and see if we can't make sense of it."

"What is it?"

"A few things. Bud went to see Stan Levinson, Daphne's camera man, and was very troubled by some of what he said or what he refused to answer. He doesn't have an alibi for the night Daphne was murdered and Bud said his explanation of why he wasn't with her was essentially nonexistent. Wants to get him in for a formal interview, which is fine, but I want us to be prepared so we have the very best chance at getting what we need."

I nodded and thought about it.

"Do you think he could be the killer?" he asked.

I shrugged. "Certainly possible, though it's just as likely if not more so that he's a copycat. Maybe he wanted Daphne dead for some reason and made it look like the Stone Cold Killer. Who knows? Be good to talk to Ernie and the others about it."

"This other thing . . ." he began. "Well, before I get to that . . . Benton Weston is back in the country and has been longer than we realized. In fact, it's possible he never left."

"What?"

"It's very confusing," he said, "but . . . his dad has essentially the same name . . . and it looks now like it was his dad who was gone or either they both were but the son came back before the dad did and we thought he was still gone when it was the dad. I don't know, but—"

"Was he back before Daphne was killed?"

"Looks like it," he said. "Thing is . . . we can't even talk to him. We can only talk to his attorney. We'd have to arrest him to talk to him and I want us to be damn sure it's him before we do that."

"But knowing he was here or possibly was . . . we can take a closer look at him."

"Which is what we're going to do starting tomorrow," he said.

"Look forward to that," I said.

"The other thing is . . ."

"*There's more*?" I asked, my voice rising.

"Yeah, and this last one is . . . You're the only one I'm telling this one to. I hope this is nothing. I really do, but . . . there's this speed dating thing like once a month. It moves to different places all over the city. The women sit at the tables and the men rotate and they talk for a few minutes, then move to the next. It's changed names a few times, but it's the same thing and it moves around the city, so . . . it took us a while to find it. It was one of the GBI agents I have sifting through the victims' lives that found it. All four victims had done it at some point."

"You sure?"

He nodded. "And . . . last spring . . . Daphne Littleton did a special report on it, so was actually at one or two of the events."

"Which means her camera man was," I said.

"Yeah, I guess it does."

"But some of our other suspects may have been too," I said. "What if Benton lied about how he met Shelly or what if Patrick Dorsey has done it?"

He nodded again, but it wasn't enthusiastically and I could tell something was bothering him. "Yes, we need to do all that, but . . . and this is the part that only you and I know for now . . . it was at one of these speed dating events that Walt met his girlfriend."

"Really?"

"Unfortunately."

"Damn," I said. "Damn. Damn. Damn."

"Yep."

"Damn. Damn."

"Exactly. So . . . tomorrow's gonna be a big day—may even be the day we break the case, so we should call it a night."

I nodded, knowing that I wouldn't be able to sleep.

Frank picked up his radio and spoke into it, "Erin, you about ready to call it a night?"

"Would like to make it an early night," she said, "but let's give it a little bit longer. Make it worth all the setup and everything."

"You just tell us when."

"Will do."

When he returned the radio to the seat beside him, I said, "I've been thinking about something else too. I think it's possible that he only used the ice stunt in the Daphne Littleton murder. Knew everyone was watching. Knew there was no way he could get down without getting caught if he was up there when she was released."

"You're probably right," he said." Though . . . could be that he likes to watch them fall from some vantage point below, set up beneath the mountain with binoculars—or even a video camera so he can watch it over and over and relive it. Fuel the fantasy."

I nodded and thought about it. He was right, and the sophistication of his thinking and the level of understanding and insight into how the killer might act or what he might do showed me just how much I had to learn.

"It would let him be with the rest of us," I said. "Like Walt was."

"God, I hope it's not him."

I then told him about Walt appearing beside us as we approached the wooded area where Daphne's camera was found. "Seemed far too fast for him to be up there if he had started at the bottom."

"You sure that's him?" Joe said on the radio. "I don't think that's him."

"You sure?" Walt said.

"We'll know for sure when he gets out of the—that's not him. Repeat it's not him. We do not have eyes on suspect. Repeat we do not have eyes on Dorsey."

"You sure?" Walt said. "Damn sure him when he left the house."

"He must've switched with someone at the restaurant. Frank, what do we do? It's not him. What do we do?"

As Frank reached for his radio, I looked up to check on Erin and saw the last of her disappearing into the wooded area next to where she had been running.

52

"Erin," I yelled into my radio. "Erin."

"Where'd she go?" Frank asked. "Was she—"

I raced up to the spot where she had disappeared, jammed the car into *Park*, and jumped out, gun in one hand, flashlight and radio held awkwardly in the other.

Without waiting for Frank, I ran into the woods near the spot where I had last seen Erin.

It was thick and dark and I had to move far more slowly than I wanted to.

The small beam of my light bounced about erratically, illuminating random spots and patches of ground and tree trunk and pine straw and hay-colored underbrush.

From somewhere back by the car Frank yelled something that may have been, "John, wait," but I couldn't be sure.

I thought I could hear panting and footfalls up ahead, but I couldn't be sure about that either.

Walt and Joe continued to talk on the radio until Frank explained what was going on and told them to get over here and call in more backup.

I turned down my radio even more and tried to concentrate,

sweeping the beam of the flashlight and the barrel of my gun all around me as I proceeded.

I realized I hadn't even remembered to look for footprints and so began searching the ground around me for them.

There were none.

Which meant I had already gone off in a different direction than they had.

I swung around to backtrack.

As I did, I lost my footing, tripped over an exposed root in the cold earth and went down.

I managed to hold onto my weapon, but had to drop my light and radio to use my left hand to catch myself.

Reaching for my light and radio, I heard Erin scream.

Jumping up and grabbing my light, I took off in the direction of the sound—or the direction I thought it had come from.

I had gone no more than ten feet before I ran into a low-hanging oak limb.

The limb struck me on the right side of my forehead and knocked me down.

Blood began trickling down into my right eye. I tried to stand as I pawed at the blood and realized just how dazed I was.

When I made it to my feet, the earth beneath me and the forest around me were spinning rapidly and I had to spread my legs and extend my arms to keep from falling down again.

"GUN," Erin yelled.

"You're a fuckin'—" Dorsey said.

"Cop," Erin said. "And you're under arrest."

I walked toward the sound, squinting to see out of my left eye and trying to get my bearings as I waited for my wits to return and my legs to start cooperating.

"Stop," Erin said. "You're under—"

A shot was fired, its report echoing through the cold quiet of the night.

Something moved to my right.

I turned in that direction and could see Dorsey running toward me, gun up.

I fired two quick shots as I dropped behind the base of a small tree for cover.

He didn't return fire and I heard him hit the ground.

My heart was pounding so hard but I couldn't tell if it was that or the cold that was making my torso quake.

After a quick but deep intake of breath, I wiped blood from my eye, leaned out the side of the tree, shone the beam of the flashlight around, searching for Dorsey.

When the small circle of light finally found the body it wasn't that of Patrick Dorsey.

I had shot Frank.

I jumped up and stumbled across toward him, falling next to where he laid face down on the ground.

Rolling him over I said, "Frank. Frank. Are you—"

"The son of a bitch shot me," he said. "Look out for—"

"It was me," I said. "I'm the son of a bitch. Where are you hit?"

"*You*?"

"Yeah. Where are you hit?"

"You shot me? Why?"

"Why do you think? I didn't like the way you were looking at me. I thought you were Dorsey. Where are you hit?"

"Just in the leg. I'm okay. What happened to your eye?"

I looked down at his legs. The bottom of his left pant leg was black with blood.

"I fired twice," I said.

"Well, you only hit me once. Thank Christ you're not a better shot."

"Shit, Frank, I'm so sorry, man."

"It's my fault. I shouldn't've been running at you like that. I tried to circle around and come in behind him, but I didn't go far enough I guess. Where is Erin? You've got to find her. Go. I'm fine.

I'm gonna make a tourniquet with my belt, but I probably don't even need that. I'm fine. Go."

"What the fuck is going on out here tonight?" Dorsey said, as he stepped up behind me and stuck the barrel of a gun into the back of my head. "Y'all shootin' each other. What the fuck is wrong with you people?"

"Put the gun down," Frank said.

"This is entrapment. What the hell kind of cops are—"

"Put the gun down," Frank said. "Where is Officer Newman? What'd you do to her?"

"*Who*? The fuck's goin' on out—"

I spun around and fired up at him. And missed.

Frank fired and hit his gun arm.

But Dorsey didn't drop his gun. Instead he lifted it up and pointed it at Frank.

And then we all fired again. Me and Frank—and Walt and Joe coming up from the left and Erin walking up from the other side of Frank.

And this time no one missed. Not even me.

Dorsey managed to get off a round but it hit the ground inches from Frank's right foot.

There was no way to tell who's shot went where but we hit Patrick Dorsey in the right side of his chest, his lower left abdomen, his right leg, his right shoulder, and his right eye.

He was dead before his mortal remains crumpled onto the cold hard ground.

53

"Who y'all think got him in the eye?" Joe said.

"Sure as shit know who it *wasn't*," Walt said, and looked at me.

Everyone laughed.

It was much, much later that night, and we were in Frank's hospital room at Dekalb Medical.

"We lucky he didn't shoot one of us," Walt said.

I felt guilty and embarrassed about shooting Frank, and this wasn't helping.

With Sylvia in the condition she was in, this was the last thing either of them needed.

"Could happen to anybody," Erin said, and patted me on the shoulder.

"Barely a scratch," Frank said.

Fortunately, the round had completely missed bone and went clean through the side of his calf muscle. Pretty much all that had been required was cleaning the wound and sewing up his leg.

"Well, I don't know about all that," Walt said, "but y'all gotten a little off topic. Pretty sure I's the one that put that round through that bastard's eye and into his brain."

I couldn't look at Walt the same now. I was trying not to let it show, but I was suspicious of him—everything he said and did.

"How you figure?" Joe asked.

"Had the angle and—"

"We had the same angle," Joe said.

"—I'm the best shot."

"Bullshit you are."

"How are you?" Frank asked Erin.

She nodded. "Okay. Wish . . . I would've been able to subdue him. Then none of this would've happened. We'd be able to question him and . . . I thought I was ready, thought I could handle myself, but . . . when he jumped me . . . I just sort of froze at first. I'm sorry, guys."

"You did great," Frank said.

"No need to apologize," I said. "Not at all. You're the reason we got him."

"Yeah," Walt said, "least you didn't shoot any of us. Only apology needed is from John to Frank."

"He's already apologized," Frank said. "Several times. But he didn't need to. It was my fault. He didn't do anything wrong. I was late coming in—I'm getting old and slow. And I ran right at him with my gun drawn right after Erin yelled that Dorsey had a gun and was getting away."

"That's true," Erin said. "It was my fault."

"No," Frank said. "You did great. You all did. But I'm serious. John didn't do anything wrong and you need to lay off him."

Walt started to say something, but stopped as Bud walked into the room.

"Great work everyone," he said. "We got him." He looked at Frank. "How you feeling, old man?"

"Can't remember when I was any better," Frank said.

Bud smiled. "Good. That's good. Glad to hear it."

"How'd it go?" Frank asked.

Bud had just finished a meeting with the FBI and GBI and gave a statement to the press.

He nodded. "Good . . . all things considered. So this is how this thing's gonna go," he added, glancing at each of us. "The FBI is going to review our case while the GBI looks into the shooting. Now look, I want you all to be cooperative. Answer all their questions that you can—fully and honestly—but take care of each other, look out for each other, as you do. Understand?"

We nodded.

He looked directly at Walt. "Understand?"

"Just as well as anyone else in here," he said.

"Frank and I've both spoken to the GBI agent handling the shooting investigation and we've decided to leave Frank's little scratch out of the public report. He's still going to investigate it, but no one beside him and the people in this room will ever know about it. Ever. That means I better not hear a peep about it ever again—not from any of you and damn sure not from the press. Understand?"

Everyone nodded.

"I mean it," Bud said. "I won't just have your job. I'll have your balls."

As if an afterthought he looked at Erin. "Sorry. Or your . . . you know what I mean."

"She got the biggest balls in the room," Walt said. "Why I've always been happy to have her as my partner."

"Thank you," I said. "Thank you all for . . ."

"You did great out there," Bud said. "What happened could've happened to anyone—especially under the circumstances. You don't need something like this following you for the rest of your career."

"Well, I really appreciate it. It means a lot to me. I've got to spend some time thinking about everything and figure out if I should even keep doing this, but . . . I can't tell you how much I . . . appreciate what y'all are doing."

"It's the least we can do," Bud said.

"It really is," Frank said. "You didn't hesitate to run in there by yourself after Erin. Who knows what might have happened if you didn't. She could be dead right now."

"I really could," she said, then looked at Walt. "So let me reiterate this too. I will fuck up anybody who says anything to anyone about what happened—especially the press. And you know I'll do it."

"Look, I'm about to take offense," Walt said. "I ain't gonna say shit to anyone. So none of y'all best single my black ass out again. *Understand* that?"

54

"You feel like talking about what happened?" Bud asked.

He was talking to Erin who was in the seat beside him. I was in the back seat. We had ridden to the hospital with Frank in the ambulance and now Bud was giving us a ride home.

"No, I don't mind. Gonna have to tomorrow to strangers anyway. I just wish we could know for sure he's our guy."

"What's your gut tell you?"

"That he is, but I . . . I'm just not positive. I'm not saying he's not. I'm just saying I can't be certain."

"What did he say to you?" I asked.

"It was incoherent," she said. "Most of it didn't make sense or at least I couldn't make sense out of it. It was menacing, threatening, but . . . I don't know . . . kind of random and like I said pretty unintelligible."

"That's interesting," Bud said. "We didn't find any rope or wood or anything."

"Really?" Erin said.

"Maybe it was in his vehicle," I said. "How'd he get there? Who was in his vehicle that Joe and Walt were following?"

"Some kid who worked at the restaurant. Patrick dates his

mom. Paid him fifty bucks to put on his hat and jacket and drive his car home. Not sure how he got to the park. Didn't find a vehicle or anything."

"He had to get a ride," I said. "It's too far for him to have walked or run and gotten there when he did."

"Or maybe he had a vehicle and we just haven't found it yet," Bud said. "But it does raise a lot of questions. It's almost like he knew exactly where to go."

"He could have," Erin said. "Someone could have tipped him off, but . . . I was the only woman jogging in the park, so it could just be that. Or . . . he could've left the restaurant long before Joe and Walt thought he did."

"True. So . . . we still have a lot of unanswered questions. Always expect to have some, but . . . want to answer all the ones we can and I damn sure don't want to tell everyone we got him and then have another girl be killed."

"That's the thing, isn't it?" Erin said. "One sure way we'll know if it was him is if they stop. If there are no more sacrifices . . . then . . ."

"Right," Bud said. "Exactly. Time will tell. But if it was him and he was tipped off . . . who the hell would do that? We're the only ones who knew you were where you were, right?"

"I can't believe that about one of my colleagues," she said, "but . . . we've involved a lot more people lately. Still . . . can't see what they'd gain from telling him and why him?"

"'Cause of how you interrogated him," Bud said.

"Okay. He had it in for me, but who would tell him?"

"Same bastard that was feeding that reporter information," he said.

"Who?" she said. "Walt? Why?"

"Maybe."

"Why would he?"

"John, you're awfully quiet back there," Bud said. "You fall asleep."

"Just thinking about everything," I said. "Especially what y'all are saying. Find it all interesting, intriguing."

"Why would Walt or anyone actually tell Patrick where I was?" Erin said. "Sic him on me like that."

And then it hit me. The most likely reason anyone would do something like that would be to deflect suspicion from themselves.

I thought about Walt again. About him appearing on the top of the mountain when he did, about him expressing interest in Daphne, about the dating service.

"He's been acting awfully strange lately," Bud said.

"He's jealous of and threatened by John," Erin said. "'Bout peed himself when he heard you accidentally shot Frank. And I'm too much of a lady to say what he about did when you said you might quit the force."

"I sure hope you won't do that," Bud said. "Please think long and hard about it, John. For our department as much as for your future. We need a mind like yours working with us."

"He's right," Erin said. "They really do. But I get it."

"Why'd you use the word *they*?" Bud asked.

"I'm not sure I have it in me anymore either," she said. "Not after tonight. Not after how I responded—or failed to—not after what might have happened. I don't . . . Just not sure I can keep doing this job after that."

"I can't lose you both," Bud said. "Please. Y'all are just exhausted and . . . you've both been through so much. Don't make any decisions yet. Give yourself some time to rest and recuperate before you do anything."

"I know what you're saying," Erin said, "but this isn't a rash decision for me. And it's not just about tonight. Mostly, but not just. Either way I think I'm gonna take a leave of absence and figure out my next move. After that I may come back if you'll have me."

"'Course I'll have you. I'll have you both. That's what I'm

saying. I want both of you to stay. Take a little time, sure, but don't quit. Y'all are too good not to be cops."

When we dropped Erin off at her little house in the town of Stone Mountain, Bud made his case for her staying once again, and only let her out of the car when she promised to take some time to think about it and not make any decisions until she talked to him again.

When I got out to walk her to her door, she shook her head. "It's sweet of you," she said, "but if you see me in, it'll only add insult to injury. Act like you were just moving to the front seat and that I'm fully capable of taking care of myself."

I smiled and nodded and said, "That's all I was doing. Didn't want the chief feeling like my chauffeur."

"Thank you, John. Get some rest and take good care of yourself. Don't let what happened tonight get you down. You were nothing short of a hero out there."

"Only one true hero out there tonight," I said. "And everybody knows who it was."

After she was in safely and we were pulling away, Bud cleared his throat and I knew a story was coming.

"In all my time as a cop," he said, "I've never had to pull my gun. Not once. Yet . . . I've fired it accidentally three different times. Three times I've accidentally discharged it and it's nothing short of miraculous that I didn't shoot anyone—myself included. Statistically there are more accidental shootings, more friendly fire shootings, by cops each year than any other kind."

I smiled. I was pretty sure he had just made that up and that it wasn't even close to true, but it made me love him and want to work for him all the more.

55

As soon as I walked into the lobby of the quiet, empty inn, I went past Summer who was seated behind the check-in desk, and directly to the bar and removed a bottle of vodka.

"Hey," she said, standing.

When I walked up to her desk, I said, "Goodnight."

"What? Wait? What happened? How are you?"

"Don't feel like talkin' about it right now."

"What happened to your eye?" she asked, reaching across the counter to touch it.

I shook my head. "It's not my eye. It's my head. It's a self-inflicted scalp laceration that bled a lot but it's fine."

She touched my cheek. "I'm worried about you. I can tell you're not in a good place. I wish you'd talk to me and not drink."

"Just been a long day," I said. "I'm tired."

"It's more than that."

I nodded. "Yes it is. I feel stupid and inept and juvenile and . . . I suck at this job. I've never been so humiliated in my entire life. I want to get drunk and I want to pass out, but what I really want is to never go in again, never see any of them again."

"Who?"

"The others. The task force."

"*What*? Why? What the hell happened?"

"You can't *intuit* it?"

"John."

"Sorry. That was . . . I'm sorry. I'm just . . . I need to be alone right now. I'm in no shape for company. Sorry again."

"Please tell me what happened."

"I shot Frank."

"Frank? Why?"

"It was an accident."

"Is he okay?"

"He's fine. He'll be fine, but . . ."

"What happened?" she asked.

I shook my head. "I can't. Not right now. I'm going to our room. Sorry again for . . ."

"It's okay. Get some rest. I wish you'd sleep instead of drink. Call me if you need anything. Anything at all."

In the room I began knocking back shots of straight vodka and pacing around thinking about the case.

I thought about Patrick Dorsey and the fact that he didn't have any of the items we'd expect the Stone Cold Killer to have—no rope, no knife, no wood, no vehicle.

I thought about him knowing exactly where Erin would be.

I thought about Walt appearing on the mountain that day and his attitude toward me.

I thought about Daphne Littleton—all the information she was able to get about the case, about her writing the letters, about the killer punishing her for her transgressions.

I thought about Benton Weston and for some reason Bobby Meredith.

I thought about the killer and what kind of man he really was, what particular kind of psychopath. Was he really making offerings on the top of the mountain? Was I right about that?

Was I right about the blocks of ice and his use of them so he could be somewhere else when Daphne was dangling off the side of the mountain? If so the killer could be anybody.

How did he get so close to Daphne? To the others? Was he in authority? Did he wear a disguise?

I thought of Ted Bundy using a fake badge, of how many killers over the years had done similar things.

Did he pretend to be a cop? Or was he a cop?

And then I began thinking about how Patrick Dorsey had acted tonight, the things he said, the things he did.

I thought about Walt saying his had been the fatal shot.

And just like that I saw it. Suddenly, all the disparate pieces of intel and information came together to form a coherent image.

Of course. It had to be. It couldn't be.

I knew or thought I knew who had told Dorsey where Erin would be.

No. No way. Couldn't be. It was too—

A tap on the door was followed by Summer walking in.

"Hey," she said. "Didn't want to startle you. I'd hoped you'd be in bed. What're you doing?"

"Drinking and thinking. Thinking and drinking. What are you doing?"

"Got somebody to cover for me so I could be with you. I was worried about you."

"I'm . . . I'll be all right."

She had a large bag or purse or something draped over her shoulder—something I'd never seen her with before.

"You didn't tell me y'all got the killer tonight," she said. "That's . . . so great. Why can't that be enough for tonight? Why can't you lay down with me and try to sleep?"

I shook my head. "'Cause," I said, and I could hear the

slightest hint of a slur. "'Cause I don't think he's the killer. I don't. I don't think he is."

"Do you know who is?" she asked.

I shrugged.

"You do, don't you?" she said. "Who? Who is it?"

"I . . . I don't know. It's too . . . I suck at this. I can't be right. It can't be who I think it is."

"Why can't it?"

I shrugged.

"You're so good at this," she said. "It's your gift—one of them anyway. You're just . . . your confidence is shot right now. You're down on yourself because of the accident tonight and the drinking's not helping."

I tried to focus.

"Are you listening to me?" she said.

I nodded.

"Forget about the stupid accident. That has nothing to do with how good you are at figuring out and solving crimes. The one has nothing to do with the other. If I was a great chef and I dropped one of my best dishes before I could serve it, that wouldn't change what a good chef I am, would it?"

I shrugged. "Guess not."

"Well? Tell me? Who is it?"

And then it hit me, a solution for testing the veracity of my other possible solution.

"What if . . . If I took you . . . If you were around him, would you sense that it's him?"

"Can't be positive, but probably, yeah. You want me to test your suspicions? Confirm for you that you're right . . . Give you the confidence to . . . act. But what if I'm wrong? What if it really is the guy and you're right and I get it wrong? What then?"

"I know I'm right," I said. "It's the only solution that fits all the evidence. It's crazy and farfetched, but it's right."

"So tell me and let's go find him so I can see if I sense anything."

"He wears a disguise," I said. "Pretends to be something that he's not. It's how he's been ahead of us this whole time, how he tricked Daphne, how he set up Patrick Dorsey."

"How? Who is it?"

56

"He's dressing up as and pretending to be a woman," I said. "It's Erin Newman."

"What?"

"Best disguise ever," I said. "Not only does he pretend to be a woman, but he's a cop—has access and knowledge and training and the trust of everyone—the victims and his fellow investigators."

"What made you—"

"What's your initial response?" I asked.

She nodded. "You're right. I'd like to be around him again, just one more time knowing what I know now, but . . . yeah. How'd you . . ."

"So many things. How plain and masculine Erin is, but how much makeup she wears. How physically strong and resilient she is. Think about the stamina required to run the way she has—night after night. Mile after mile. She's like a machine. Think of the irony of us using her, a runner like her to catch a runner like him. We knew someone inside the investigation was feeding Daphne Littleton information. I thought it was Walt. He thought it was me. But it was her. She gained her trust—the way she did so many people's—including mine. And she's always wearing that damn turtleneck under her uniform. My guess it's to hide her Adam's apple."

Summer shook her head. "Oh my God. You're right. You're absolutely right."

"One of the biggest clues was her saying she saw the killer up on the mountain when Daphne was hanging from the rope. She said she saw part of his arm disappearing behind the boulder into the woods, but he wasn't up there—no one was. He had rigged it with the blocks of ice so he didn't have to be up there when she was dangling off the mountain. He did that so he could be with us. What a perfect alibi. Hell, he's the one who came to our room that morning to get me, remember?"

"Of course I do. That was the morning after we first made love."

"Yes, it was. That was such a—"

"Go ahead," she said. "What else?"

"When Frank offered for her to stop tonight, she said she wanted to go a little longer—because she knew Patrick Dorsey was coming. She also ran on the south side by the old quarry tonight—something she's never done before. In the interview when she asked Patrick if she made him nervous, he said *no*. He was telling the truth. Women make him nervous. She's not a woman. I don't know what she said to him to get him out there tonight, but he was so confused about what was going on. Called it entrapment. Asked what kind of cops we were. I don't know if he touched her or what happened, but he shouted *You're a*—and I think he was going to say *man*, but she yelled *cop* real loud to cover it up, then fired her gun. He ran and she yelled to us that he was armed so we'd shoot him. And if we didn't, she was going to. I'll bet you anything she's the one who hit him in the eye."

Summer continued to shake her head.

"Walt and Bud and the rest of them are always teasing about how she's stronger and braver and tougher than any man on the force. Even tonight in Frank's room they were teasing about the size of her balls. On the ride back to her house tonight, she told Bud she was going to quit, or at least take a leave of absence. She had set up Dorsey—I guarantee there are items of clothing from the victims in his house—and she's going to move on, so the murders will stop here and everyone will think it was Dorsey. And she can start making her sacrifices somewhere else. She even used that term tonight. *Sacrifices.* It's just a theory I had. Not many of the other guys have called them that. They keep referring to them as *murders*, but he couldn't. He used *sacrifices* with conviction and certainty because that's what he's been making."

"Is he a man or a woman or a man trying to be a woman?"

I shook my head. "Erin is just his cover. It's a disguise. His way of appearing normal in the world. I bet it's far easier to play a sane woman than try to keep it together as himself. He's just playing a part every day."

"You're a genius, John Jordan," she said. "How are we gonna get close to him so I can confirm you're right?"

"I say we drive over to his house right now," I said.

"I say that's the liquor talking, but go on."

"I tell him I couldn't sleep, had a few more questions about what Dorsey did out there in the woods. We stay for just a few minutes, then leave. And either you confirm what I'm thinking or I start over."

57

When the door opened at Erin's house it wasn't Erin at all, but the madman who had been making sacrifices on Stone Mountain.

And he was pointing a sawed-off shotgun at me.

Summer and I both held our hands up.

"Come in," he said, his voice different and deeper than anything that had ever come out of Erin's mouth before.

I turned to Summer. "Sorry," I said. "This was stupid."

I couldn't believe I had brought her here like this. I was even worse at this than I thought I was.

"I said, come in," he said, pulling back the hammer on the shotgun.

We did.

"What's your real name?" I asked.

"Aaron," he said. "Like Moses' brother, the priest. I'm the new Aaron, a priest who offers sacrifices to God."

"Erin Newman," I said.

Summer said, "I can confirm your suspicion. He's the killer."

I laughed. I couldn't help it. "Thanks."

"Anything else you want to know about me or my work before you die?" he asked me.

I thought about it. "Can't think of anything," I said.

"You couldn't understand anyway," he said.

And then he shot me. Twice.

As I fell backwards and hit the ground, I saw him grab Summer and drag her away. It was the last thing I saw before everything went dark and I lost consciousness.

58

He had time for one more sacrifice before he left. Why not. It's not like they're looking for him.

From what he knew of this one she needed to be offered up as a sin offering to the Most High.

She wasn't just a whore—shacking up with John in their hotel room of sin—but she was a witch too, a worshiper of Satan.

A man also or woman that hath a familiar spirit, or that is a wizard, shall surely be put to death: they shall stone them with stones: their blood shall be upon them.

He bound her wrists and ankles and taped her mouth shut with a gag, then threw her in the back of his car and covered her with a tarp.

It was dark. No one was watching the mountain. If he timed it just right he could make his final offering on this sacred site just as the sun was rising in the east.

This would be both an end and a beginning for him, an alpha and omega on the holy mount of the Lord of Hosts.

59

Blinking my eyes open I felt the most intense pain I had ever experienced.

I was lying in a pool of my own blood.

It took a while, but I managed to sit up.

Seeing what looked like the victims' clothes in a nearby suitcase, I crawled over to it and began using jogging pants and shirts and jackets to make compression wraps for my chest and abdomen in an attempt to slow the bleeding.

I could tell from the shot pattern that one of the rounds had been birdshot and one had been buckshot. I was bleeding from the myriad pellets imbedded in my chest and arms, but the real damage, severest pain, and greatest blood loss came from the single slug that had ripped through the side of my abdomen. Thankfully, it had actually ripped all the way through me—I could feel blood seeping out of the exit wound in the back. And the fact that I was still here and able to somewhat function, meant it must have missed most or even all of my major organs. Still, the blood loss alone would kill me soon if it wasn't stopped.

I scanned the small, cluttered room for a phone.

There was one on a small table by a chair in the corner.

Pushing myself up, I fell forward over toward it and snatched up the receiver.

I couldn't call Frank. He was still in the hospital. I didn't know Bud's number. All I could do was call the dispatcher and tell her what had happened and where I thought Aaron would be taking Summer.

After I managed that, I stumbled out the door and to my car and drove toward the park, unable to turn my head or upper body as I did.

I had to save her. I couldn't let her die the way I had Jordan.

Driving through the gate at the entrance to the park, I didn't stop, didn't really even slow down, but I did yell out my window for the confused and angry attendant to call the police, that it was an emergency.

I found Aaron's car parked near the entrance to the walk-up trail and screeched to a stop beside it.

Climbing out slowly, I willed myself to climb the mountain and save Summer—even if it killed me.

As I began making my way up the slope I felt supported and encouraged and aided by the clothes tied tightly around my chest, the clothes that had once belonged to Cheryl Carver, Pamela Nichols, Shelly Hepola, and Kathy Dady.

It was dark and cold.

I was exhausted and hungover and shot up.

I had lost a lot of blood and was dizzy and lightheaded.

Every step hurt.

My makeshift tourniquet seemed to be working. I didn't appear to be bleeding as much.

Of course it could just be that I had less blood left to bleed.

As I continued my slow and awkward ascent, I either began to loosen up some or learned better how to move to minimize my pain or both, but I was beginning to move better and faster.

I still expected to get overtaken at any time by other cops and emergency workers responding to my call to the dispatcher or my plea to the gate attendant.

I couldn't be sure how far I had climbed, but I was certain it wasn't nearly as far as it felt.

Everything in me but the most important thing told me to stop, to rest, to take a short break, but I wasn't going to stop—not until I reached the top, not until Summer was safe in my arms again.

I was climbing east, and in the sky before me above the dome of the mountain of stone, the first glow of false dawn shone like a trick of light.

I continued.

Slowly.

Awkwardly.

Deliriously.

But steadily.

Stumbling and tripping, I tried my best not to fall. I was afraid if I did, if I actually went down I wouldn't be able to get back up again no matter how hard I tried, no matter how much I willed my body to do so.

Time dragged by.

Step by step.

Stumble by stumble.

I made progress.

As I neared the top, and the eastern horizon broke open its plumb-colored bruise to birth a starburst of bright brilliant orange, I could hear sirens screaming below.

When I finally reached the top I began searching for any sign of Aaron and Summer.

There was no sign of them.

Had I been wrong? Is this not where he brought her? Did he park his car below and then go in a different direction?

I seriously doubted it. I'd bet my and Summer's life, and that was what I was doing, that this was where he'd bring her, that he would be powerless not to do so.

And then out of the corner of my left eye I saw him.

On the edge of the dome overlooking the north face, he was standing there holding Summer up close to him, saying something to her as he shook her.

I stumbled toward them.

When I got close enough, he turned toward me.

"How does it feel?" he asked.

Summer looked like someone who knew she was about to die. She moaned beneath the tape covering her mouth, but it was her eyes that showed her true terror and hopeless resignation.

"What?" I said.

"To die. To be dead. To know there's nothing you can do to stop me from ending the life of this woman you care about right in front of you."

"Please," I said. "Show mercy."

He shook his head. "There is no such thing. There is only the rod. Only the knife. Only the fire. Only the fall."

"Offer me instead. Let her go."

"This was written in the great book of life before any of us were ever born," he said. "She is going to die. You are going to watch. Then you are going to die. And there's nothing you can do about it. Nothing. This is fate. This is futility. This is what everything comes to in the end. Can you see it?"

As he talked I continued to edge toward him, easing closer and closer, hoping if nothing else to be able to grab the rope curled up around them.

"When I do it," he said, "I'm not going to count to anything. I'm not going to make any pronouncements. I'm just going to do it. One moment she'll be here, the other she'll be gone. Dead and gone. And there's not a thing you can do about it. Tell me. How does that make you feel?"

"Please," I said again. "Please let her go. You've sacrificed enough."

"It's never enough."

"The same Bible that speaks of sacrifice says, 'For I desired mercy, and not sacrifice; and the knowledge of God more than burnt offerings.' Hosea six-six. God is a God of compassion. His mercies are new every morning."

"That's true," he said, nodding and looking contemplative.

He then flung her off the side of the mountain.

I dove for the end of the rope, but couldn't reach it.

As I pushed myself up and reached for the rope again, all I could do was watch it unspool and disappear off the side of the mountain with her.

He stood there with such a peaceful expression on his face as he watched the last of the rope disappear.

And then, with full knowledge of what I was doing, I lowered my shoulder and ran at him as hard and fast as I could, feeling something inside my chest tearing and ripping, ramming into him while he was still looking after his last victim, and sending him flying off the side of the mountain like all the young women he had delivered the exact same fate to.

And in that moment I was as much a murderer as he was.

Then and for the rest of my life I would have blood on my hands that no amount of scrubbing would ever get off.

And then I did the only thing left for me to do, the only thing I could do.

I collapsed and began to cry, waiting to see if I would bleed out and die up here or if help might arrive in time.

And just then I couldn't say I truly preferred one eventuality over the other.

60

The first time I opened my eyes in the hospital room I was alone.

The second time a nurse was present.

She told me there had been people with me around the clock for days and that I just happened to regain consciousness when none of them were here—a true rarity according to her.

At various times of fading in and out of awareness over the next few days, I saw a variety of people in my room, including Susan, Susan's aunt Margaret, Merrill, my parents, Frank, Don Paulk and some of my professors from EPI, Bud, Miss Ida and some of the members from the Missing and Murdered Children group.

One time I thought I saw Anna and her new husband Chris Taunton, but couldn't be sure about that. Could've easily dreamt or hallucinated it.

During all this time each in his or her own way expressed care and concern, told me how lucky I was to be alive and various facts that had come out or been uncovered about the killer.

But I wasn't interested.

I wasn't interested in anything. Usually when a case had

reached a conclusion I wanted to know as much as I could, tried to answer all the little questions—like why Patrick Dorsey attended the funeral of one of the victims or if Benton Weston had really been out of the country, or why Stan the Camera Man had acted so suspicious, or why Walt had taken such a dislike to me, and if Erin had been behind it all, but I wasn't the least bit interested in any of it.

I had no appetite. Not for anything.

I had no curiosity. No wonder.

I had no sense of taste—all the food I consumed during that time, what little there was of it, was all texture and no taste.

Similarly I had no taste for information about Aaron or how he pulled off what he did or how he had done it before in other locations.

I didn't care.

What did it matter? What would it change?

I sincerely wished he hadn't done what he had, that he hadn't stolen identities and changed names, and offered sacrifices, but there was nothing I could do about it now.

They told me how his mother had been a sexual sadist who ran a traveling religious theater company, how in addition to torturing her two sons she had taught them how to perform, how to disappear into a role, to become the part they were playing, how to fake everything from fingerprints to the norms of human interaction.

I remembered asking how he had faked his fingerprints to get the SMPD job and being told the key was stealing the identity of someone who had never been printed before—something true of Aaron himself also.

They told me how the most popular play his mother's theater company had performed around the country was that of Abraham and Isaac on Mount Moriah. They told me how his mom had killed his brother and how he had killed his mom, but I truly didn't care.

Maybe if I had saved Summer I'd feel differently. Maybe.

But right now I didn't care about anything and I had no idea how to change that even if I had cared to, which, of course, I didn't.

"Did you love her?" Susan asked. "Sorry. Don't answer that."

I didn't respond.

"I'm gonna go soon," she said. "Just had to make sure you were going to be okay. Now that you're awake more and they say you're gonna recover, I'll . . . I won't intrude."

I started to say something, but before I could she started speaking again.

"I know I love you more than you love me—or maybe in a whole different way, but . . . I just want you to know that . . . I'm okay with that. I really am. I figure that's the way with a whole lot of relationships that seem to work. I mean . . . what are the chances two people could feel the exact same way about each other, right? Anyway, what I'm tryin' to say is . . . I'm gonna leave you alone now, but if you ever change your mind and want to give us another try . . . I'd be game—even knowing what I know."

Hearing her say that broke my busted and bruised heart all over again and made me want to love her the way she deserved.

I closed my eyes for a moment but it must have been far more because when I opened them again Merrill was sitting where Susan had been.

"You hear me?" he was saying. "My black ass drove three hundred miles up here to tell you that."

"What?" I managed to ask.

"For you not to give a fuck what anyone says or what the papers print. They can't know. No one can. Fuck 'em. You the man. You. You did what none of them could ever do."

I tried to nod.

"I know you," he said. "Sure, you don't give a damn about anything right now, but you will again—and sooner than you think. You gonna do that thing you do and you gonna care too much, care what was said, care what you did or didn't do, so what I'm tellin' you is for then far more than now. Do yourself a favor and give less of a damn. Lock all this shit in a box and bury it somewhere and for fuck sake don't ever dig it up. You feel me?"

The next time I opened my eyes, Frank was there talking.

"None of that matters," he said. "None of it. But I'll tell you what does. You put down the madman. You're one hell of an investigator and you're going to have an amazing career, but no matter what else you do . . . you'll always be the man who . . . uncovered the Stone Cold Killer. Always. Not many of the very best and experienced law enforcement officers in the world can say something like that. Doesn't matter how or . . . Doesn't matter what happened up there. You're the only person on the planet that knows and it's my hope you'll keep it that way."

I nodded and knew in that moment that was exactly what I was going to do.

"You know how much I . . ." he began. "How much I love my family. They are my . . . everything. Since you've been up here . . . several times over the years I . . . I felt like you were part of my . . . You've felt like a son to me. My own boy is . . . well, he's my heart and soul. And I . . . I just want to say—to try to tell you that . . . nothin' would make me happier than . . . than if he grew up to be just like you."

That made me cry in my sleep. I had no idea what I did awake. Thankfully.

The next time I opened my eyes—or remembered opening them—less cobwebs covered my brain, and I had a mental awareness and clarity I hadn't had since before I had been shot.

This time, dressed far more casually than before, Frank was there with his wife, who smiled and attempted to comfort me, though her face was pale, her hair thin and wispy, her body brittle and frail.

"I'm so glad you're still with us," Sylvia said.

I smiled up at her. "I'm glad we both are."

"I don't plan on going anywhere anytime soon," she said. "What about you?"

I shook my head. "No ma'am. Me either."

She reached down with her cold, bony hand and tenderly touched my cheek. "I'm gonna go sit down in the waiting room and read while y'all talk but I had to come in and tell you you're in my prayers and you can expect some good home cooking when you get out of here."

"Thank you."

Frank saw her to the door then came back and said, "You seem a lot better."

I nodded. "I am."

"Been pretty foggy," he said. "What do you remember?"

"Not much."

I tried to sit up some, but the searing pain in my abdomen and side dissuaded me. I could feel my skin going clammy and the contents of my stomach rising up my throat.

"Do you remember what I told you about the other victim or the killer?"

I shook my head, swallowing hard against the bile. "What other victim?"

"You don't remember any of it?"

"No. What other victim?"

"We found another body," he said. "It had gotten lodged on the carving."

"Since when?"

"About a week."

"How long have I been in here?" I asked.

"Three days."

"Who was she?"

"Young woman who lived in the little town of Stone Mountain," he said. "Celine Patton. She wasn't running in the park. We think he picked her up in town. You okay? You look like you might . . . be sick."

I nodded. "It's passing."

"Want some ice water?"

I nodded again. "Thanks."

He lifted the small plastic pitcher from the hospital table and poured ice and water into the little plastic cup, the flexible straw twirling around in it as he did.

He handed me the cup and I drank slowly from the straw, the cool water settling my roiling stomach almost immediately.

"What about Aaron?" I asked.

"We'll talk later," he said. "When you feel better. I just . . . It's just that I didn't want you hearing it from anyone else."

"What?" I asked. "I'm fine. Tell me."

"We found Summer's body near where we expected it to be," he said, "but . . . we still haven't found Aaron's. Are you sure he went off the side of the mountain?"

"What? Positive. His body should be very close to where Summer's was. Are you sure it's not—"

"We're still searching," he said. "Who knows? Maybe—"

"You haven't found him?" I said. "Are you—Did you look in the trees? Maybe he got hung up in the trees like Daphne."

"We've looked," he said.

"He went over too far away from the monument to get caught in it, but what about an outcropping or—"

"We've had rock climbers and helicopters and everything else searching the entire area," he said. "We've been looking for traces of blood or anything—was he injured before going off the mountain?"

I shook my head.

"He probably got caught on something," he said. "We're still looking. We'll find him."

"He could've gotten caught on a boulder or outcropping or something and survived," I said. "What if he caught himself and climbed back up or . . ."

"Even if he did, which I doubt it . . . the park is closed. We've got the place surrounded, exits blocked, armed search teams combing every inch of the—we'll find him. I just wanted you to know. But I don't want you to worry. We'll find him. And in the meantime we've got an officer posted right outside your door, so rest easy. You're safe."

"I don't care about that," I said. "I just care about that bastard being off the board. I thought he was."

"He is. I'm sure. Don't worry about it. Don't worry about a thing. Just get better. I'll come and tell you the minute we find him. Okay?"

But when I got out four days later, he had not been back to tell me because they still hadn't found him, and I didn't know of anyone who seriously believed they still would.

61

The moment I opened the door of Scarlett's, I knew something was wrong.

A quick glance around told me nothing and everything had changed.

And it wasn't just that there wasn't a single customer in the joint, and I had never seen it when at least a couple of regulars weren't present, though that was certainly disconcerting.

I was here looking for Susan.

When I had been released from the hospital and returned to our old rented farmhouse on Flakes Mill Road, not only was she not there, but none of her things were either.

Days had passed with no word from her. I had no idea where she was or how to get in touch with her—except of course here at Scarlett's or through her Aunt Margaret. I had decided to come in person instead of calling.

I should have called.

I didn't recognize the young man behind the bar. And in fact had never seen a man behind the bar before.

My heart sank a little more into the hollowness of my soul beneath it at not seeing Susan or Margaret.

I wasn't even sure what I wanted, didn't know what I would say, but I longed for connection, to at least reestablish contact and . . . what? See if I couldn't love Susan like she deserved?

"What can I getcha?" the young bartender asked.

"I was looking for Susan," I said.

"Who?"

"The other bartender," I said. "Margaret's niece."

"Oh. I met Margaret. I didn't meet her niece. Margaret used to own this place. She sold it to my dad last week. Sorry, don't really know much else besides that. My dad might. He'll be here tomorrow during the day."

"Thanks."

As I turned to leave, the door opened.

In the moment it took for my eyes to adjust I experienced a fraction of a second of hope that it might be Susan or at least Margaret.

It wasn't.

It was Frank Morgan and I was happy to see him.

"Thought I might find you here," he said.

He stopped abruptly and looked around. "What's different?"

"Everything," I said. "Margaret sold the place. They're gone—Susan, Margaret, all the regulars."

"What're you doing here?" he asked.

"Looking for them. Just found out."

"Damn. That's got to be a blow. Buy you a cup of coffee?"

I nodded. "Thanks."

We turned toward the young man behind the bar.

He shook his head. "No coffee, I'm afraid. Y'all want a beer or something?"

"Thanks anyway," I said. "Good luck with this place. If Margaret or Susan come in, please let them know that John Jordan is looking for them."

Frank and I stepped outside onto the little porch of the storefront strip mall.

It was a crisp, cool, clear evening, the headlights of the cars on Memorial Drive beginning to blink on in the expansive gloaming.

As we stood there together, I thought again about how nearly everyone I was close with was older than me—most by a good bit—and wondered again at what that meant.

"How are you feeling?" I asked.

He nodded. "I'm good."

"Sorry again for shooting you."

"How are you doing?" he asked.

I shrugged, keeping my gaze on the passing traffic. "To be honest I don't feel like myself."

"I'm sure you're still in shock—and not just physically. What you went through . . ." he added, letting it hang there in the cold, dim air between us.

"I was hoping Susan could help," I said, "but . . . it's probably best she wasn't here. I was already feeling guilty. Don't want to use her to . . . try to feel . . . something other than . . . what I'm feeling."

"Are you sleeping?"

"Not a lot," I said, "but . . . never have."

"You thinking Aaron might come for you?"

I shrugged.

As of two days ago, the searches had been called off and the park had been reopened. No body had been found. I had tried to kill the madman and had failed. Of course, he had tried to kill me and failed too.

"I wish he would," I said, and I meant it, but not in the way it sounded. It had nothing to do with bravado and everything to do with wanting this to be over—no matter the final outcome. "But I'm sure he won't as long as you have agents watching me twenty-four hours a day."

He smiled. "Told them to try not to be seen. How long have you known?"

"They followed me home from the hospital," I said. "I was looking over my shoulder for Aaron and saw them."

"I'd like to catch him, but I sleep better at night knowing you're safe."

I felt something hard inside my chest dissolve a little and I had to blink several times.

"Thank you, Frank," I said. "That means . . . a lot."

He had asked me repeatedly to move in with him, but I couldn't put him or his family in danger—especially after what they had been through lately.

"We'll have people at Summer's funeral," he said. "Just in case he shows."

"He won't," I said, shaking my head.

"Well . . . just in case. Sorry to have to have agents at her . . ."

"She'd like nothing better than to have him caught there," I said. "But it's not gonna happen."

"You think we've heard the last from him?"

I shook my head again. "For a while, maybe, but not for good."

He nodded and twisted his lips into a frown. "Far worse knowing he's out there and might be coming for us than searching for a nameless, faceless killer in a case, isn't it?"

The truth was Aaron wouldn't be coming for *us*. He'd be coming for me. And there was no *might* to it. He would be coming. Maybe not today or tomorrow. But certainly and eventually and the certitude of that eventuality cast a shadow over every aspect of my existence.

"Yes, it is," I said. "It most certainly is."

ALSO BY MICHAEL LISTER

Join Michael's Readers' Group and receive 4 FREE Books!

Books by Michael Lister

Sign up for Michael's newsletter by clicking here or go to

www.MichaelLister.com and receive a free book.

(John Jordan Novels)

Power in the Blood

Blood of the Lamb

Flesh and Blood

(Special Introduction by Margaret Coel)

The Body and the Blood

Blood Sacrifice

Rivers to Blood

Innocent Blood

(Special Introduction by Michael Connelly)

Blood Money Blood Moon

Blood Cries

Blood Oath

Blood Work

Cold Blood

Blood Betrayal

Blood Shot

Blood Ties

Blood Trail

(Jimmy "Soldier" Riley Novels)

The Big Goodbye

The Big Beyond

The Big Hello

The Big Bout

The Big Blast

In a Spider's Web (short story)

The Big Book of Noir

(Merrick McKnight / Reggie Summers Novels)

Thunder Beach

A Certain Retribution

(Remington James Novels)

Double Exposure

(includes intro by Michael Connelly)

Separation Anxiety

Blood Shot

(Sam Michaels / Daniel Davis Novels)

Burnt Offerings

Separation Anxiety

Blood Oath

Blood Shot

(Love Stories)

Carrie's Gift

(Short Story Collections)

North Florida Noir

Florida Heat Wave

Delta Blues

Another Quiet Night in Desperation

(The Meaning Series)

Meaning Every Moment

The Meaning of Life in Movies

Sign up for Michael's newsletter by clicking here or go to

www.MichaelLister.com and receive a free book.